BRIAN
A MONTANA BOUNTY HUNTERS STORY

DELILAH DEVLIN

DEDICATION

I owe a debt of gratitude to Fedora Chen and fabulous author Reina Torres, whose friendship and support made it possible for me to bring you this book. Thanks, ladies!

ABOUT THE BOOK

MONTANA BOUNTY HUNTERS:
Authentic Men... Real Adventures...

Physical Therapist, Raydeen Pickering, has seen her fill of stubborn veterans, some too angry to get on with their lives, some still living in hell in their minds, and then some unwilling to let their broken bodies hold them back. She hasn't figured out which Brian Cobb is yet. The first time she met the handsome, wheelchair-bound man, he was wary and defensive, his gaze always sliding toward the door, looking for a quick escape from the Soldiers' Sanctuary meetings.

Even now, there's something about the ex-Army MP, now bounty hunter wrangler, that sets him apart from the other men she's helped mend. There's something more—not just the haunted look in his eyes or the still set of his shoulders. The way he looks at her when he thinks her attention is elsewhere gives her hope that she'll reach him, and that he'll let her help him regain more of what he's lost.

First though, he has to figure out he's in love with the

wrong woman. The one he needs is right here, and if she has to do the chasing, so be it, because those looks he gives her have rekindled a fire she thought was lost forever...

BRIAN

A MONTANA BOUNTY HUNTERS STORY

New York Times and *USA Today* Bestselling Author
Delilah Devlin

CHAPTER 1

Sweat trickled down the sides of Brian Cobb's face. His helmet felt heavy on his head, his pack dragged on his shoulders, and his boots were so hot he was walking in pools of water. The transport vehicles his squad had been promised hadn't arrived, so they were hoofing it back to camp with half a dozen prisoners chained in a line. Still, their plight was better than the infantry platoon's they'd left a click back. Once they'd given the ISIS fighters into Military Police custody, they'd headed back to continue their sweep for insurgents hiding inside the village with the unpronounceable name.

"Hey, Corncob," Private First Class Benny Sanders said as he walked beside him.

"You know I hate that nickname, Sanders," Brian muttered.

"Yeah, I do," he said, his smile stretching across his dark face. Benny jerked his chin toward the slender figure striding ahead of the chained prisoners, her dog Tessa walking, unleashed by her side. "I see how you look at her. Are you and she...?"

Brian gave Benny a glare. "No. We're just friends."

"She have a boyfriend back in the States or something?"

"No, not that it's any of your business."

"Huh. Just thought since you two spend so much time together..."

Brian shook his head. "We're friends. We hang. That's all." Not that he would mind if their friendship grew into something more. He'd had a thing for Jamie Burke since they'd met during their first drill together back in Kalispell, for what felt like eons ago. Jamie was certainly easy on the eyes with her wheat-blonde hair, lightly tanned skin, and golden-brown eyes.

However much he might have wished it otherwise, Jamie had assigned him to the "friend zone"—and because he valued their friendship, he'd never acted upon his attraction. Perhaps once they were back Stateside, he'd work up the courage to ask her out.

He'd played a multitude of scenarios in his mind of how he'd go about doing it without blowing their friendship to hell should she shoot him down. Not one of them felt like the right fit. Sure, they had lots in common—they loved playing basketball and

BRIAN

soccer, liked working out, liked animals, were both from western Montana...

Well, maybe they didn't have that much in common, but they could certainly build on what they shared now. Maybe he needed to figure out what she liked to do outside of the military, what her hobbies were, whether she liked to dance.

He liked to dance. He could imagine asking her out for a beer, just buddies going for a drink together. The music would start up, and he'd hike an eyebrow. She'd give him a laugh and say something like, "If you don't mind me stepping all over your toes," and he'd lead her to the floor. Once he held her in his arms, maybe then she'd see him as someone she could consider as dating material...

Ahead, Tessa gave a whine and moved away from Jamie, her nose going to the ground as she searched the trail they walked, moving from one side to the other.

They'd left the village and were following a well-traveled trail that led through rocky hills. The area had been cleared of enemy combatants, so they'd been ordered to march the prisoners back. Still, the danger didn't have to come from a sniper on a hilltop.

Jamie held up her closed fist, and the squad drew to a halt. Brian looked to his left. "Benny, keep an eye out," he said, indicating the hills behind them.

The squad leader, Sergeant Milligan, strode up to Jamie. "What's the holdup, Burke?"

"Don't know yet, Sarge," she said. "Tessa hasn't indicated yet."

Tessa moved ahead of the formation but lifted her nose from the trail and ran back to Jamie, her tail wagging.

Tessa reached down to give her a pat. "Must have had a whiff of something, but I think we're cool to move on."

However, Tessa gave another whine and sniffed the air. A moment later, she left Jamie's side again, this time heading down the row of prisoners toward Brian, her nose to the ground, sniffing the trail then moving slightly off it to Brian's right. She whined and moved closer to Brian.

Brian glanced around him. Tessa was a trained bomb dog. An IED might be nearby. But where? The rocky outcropping beside him caught his eye.

"Cobb!" Benny whispered.

He turned to glance at Benny, whose eyes were large. He tilted his head toward a hillside in the distance. Brian didn't glance at it directly. "You see something?"

"A glint. Then some movement. Might be one tango."

Brian had a bad feeling. "Jamie, call your dog back," he said, keeping his voice natural, "I think we've got company."

Sergeant Milligan began moving his way. Brian smiled and shook his head, trying to act like his heart wasn't racing and his stomach hadn't dropped to his boots. "Better keep back, Sarge," he said, keeping his tone carefree. "I think there's an IED in the rocks beside me, and Benny spotted movement at your three o'clock."

The sergeant's gaze betrayed his concern. "We have his buddies chained in a line. Maybe he actually gives a shit about them. How about you move forward, Cobb? Sanders," he said, calling out to Benny, giving them both a strained smile. "You move, too. Get his friends between you and him. But move slow and natural. Don't let him know we know he's there."

Although every one of the squad members was now aware of the threat, they began to patter.

"Man, I can't wait to get back to my bunk. Mama sent brownies. Got a few left."

"No, you don't, Packer. I snuck the last one when you were showering."

"Shithead, you better not have."

"Hey, Tessa," Jamie called to her dog, indicating with a finger toward the ground that Tessa should move back to her side.

The dog ran back, turned in a neat circle, and sat beside her feet. Jamie's gaze went to Brian. Her eyes were wide with fear, and her gaze shifted toward the rocks as she said, "Brian, you and I have a rematch to play against Pike and Sherman. Better hurry your ass up."

Brian gave her a crooked grin, took a deep breath, and stepped out.

A shot sounded, and Benny dropped to his knees, his head sagging toward his chest.

Brian took another step, but sound exploded then went suddenly muffled. He felt something hammer against his lower body, felt searing pain, then he was flying, everything moving in slow motion, clumps of dirt and flares of fire, tumbling head over heels until he dropped with a sickening thud on the trail.

He couldn't hear voices, but he saw movement—Sergeant Milligan pointing toward the hill and signaling for two men to move out and engage with the sniper; Pike kneeling beside Benny, who still knelt on his knees, blood gurgling from his chest.

Jamie's face entered his vision. Tears filled her eyes.

"I'm okay," he shouted, then pointed at his ears. "Can't hear though. And I'm feelin' a little...dizzy." Okay, a lot, but he didn't want to worry her.

Sergeant Milligan knelt beside Jamie, talking into his radio. Someone else moved to the opposite side of him...Kinsey, the medic. His back was to Brian as he leaned over his body.

Brian tried to get up on his elbows to tell him the problem wasn't with his legs; it was with his head, he couldn't hear, but then he glanced downward, past Kinsey.

His boots were gone. Then he realized...*so were the feet that had been sweating inside them.*

He drew a deep breath and glanced up at Jamie.

She was mouthing words he couldn't hear,

cupping his cheeks. When she bent and kissed his cheek, he knew he was dead. "I'm not fucking dying," he tried to shout, but he knew it came out a whisper, because he was weakening, barely able to keep his eyes open.

The wind pulsed against his face, and he opened his eyes, saw the helicopter above, a fiery trail of rounds blasting toward the hill before it wobbled in the air then settled on the sand beside the trail.

He raised a hand to point toward Benny. "Him first," he said, glancing sideways, but Benny was no longer kneeling. He lay with his eyes open, staring up at the cloudless blue sky.

Kinsey moved away, and Brian glanced down. Tourniquets were on his legs, below his knees. He glanced at Jamie. "They find my boots?"

Her face crumpled, and Tessa wiggled her way in between Jamie and Sergeant Milligan. Her tongue lapped at his cheek. Her cold, wet nose nuzzled his ear.

Any other time, he would have pushed her away, but Brian no longer had the strength. "Hey...they find my boots?"

BRIAN AWOKE, surprised to see darkness when the sky had just been so blue, and uncomfortably aware that the air inside his bedroom was frosty-cold not fry-an-egg-on-a-rock hot.

His words echoed in his brain once more. Those

damn, stupid boots...

Drawing in a deep breath, he pushed aside the dream, trying to remember that he'd been the lucky one. Benny had been dead the second he'd knelt in the dirt.

Brian ground his teeth together. He'd never have that chance to ask Jamie to dance, and now, Jamie was married to Sky. Not that he'd stewed for long about his lost opportunity after "the incident." He'd had too many other challenges to overcome.

Knowing he wouldn't be able to go back to sleep again—he never did after having the nightmare—he reached to the right and flicked on the switch for his bedside lamp. Then he pushed himself up to sit and swung his legs over the side of the mattress. *Almost there.*

Reaching out, he planted his right hand in the far side of his wheelchair seat, his left in the mattress beside his hip and pushed his body up and across to the edge of the seat. Settling backward on the cushion, he unlocked the wheels and made his way to the toilet in the bathroom, transferred from his chair to the toilet seat, took care of business, moved back into the chair, wheeled to the sink to wash his hands, then made his way back into his bedroom to dress.

Half an hour later, he wheeled down the hallway that led from his apartment in the back of the office building into the kitchen, pausing along the way at the thermostat on the wall to reset the temperature to a comfortable sixty-eight degrees. Thankfully, his apartment and the rest of the office were wheel-chair friendly, so the thermostat was well within his reach.

Once in the kitchen, he started the coffee machine, grabbed a bagel from the fridge, and popped it into the toaster. With a buttered bagel and a cup of coffee balanced on a tray in his lap, he moved out into the bullpen toward his desk.

He might as well get started on the day, pull a spreadsheet of skips, check his email. A million things he needed to do other than think about the fact Raydeen would be expecting him on the track at ten AM, along with all the available hunters. She'd informed him he was necessary, that they needed a timekeeper, but he knew she had ulterior motives for getting him out on the track.

She'd cajoled him more than a few times to wheel around the track to get some upper body exercise in, but him getting some cardio in wasn't what she really wanted, either. She wanted him to watch all his buddies running around the track, to remind him that he was wheelchair bound—by his own choice—but that there were other choices he could make.

She was a physical therapist, and he thought maybe she believed it was her mission in life to "fix" him—Brian Cobb. He was her challenge.

Brian didn't want to run a stopwatch for his friends. Didn't want to sit and watch them running around the track, complaining about aching joints and wheezing because they weren't in top shape. Not after a long, cold winter of sitting on their asses.

Which wasn't exactly fair, because they were all a pretty fit bunch, but he liked to gripe, at least in his mind, because while they weren't purposely cruel, their very fitness ate at his pride. Reminded him of everything he'd lost.

He rolled backwards, away from his desk, and headed to the large bulletin board at one side of the room—at the "hall of shame" pictures the group hung to celebrate their team members' most inglorious moments.

There was the pink, sequined and glittered frame surrounding the picture of Dagger and Lacey, when they'd been prom king and queen in high school; the picture of Animal confronting the bear, his arms outstretched and looking like a lunatic; another of the mud-splattered hunters who had surrounded Jamie and Sky as they'd stood in front of Reaper (who'd gotten his license to marry them over the internet) to say their vows. He hadn't been there to witness Animal's crazy act or Jamie's wedding. He'd been right here, as always, stuck hearing about everyone's adventures while his dreams rotted in this chair.

Brian leaned back his head and breathed deeply. He'd promised himself when he'd taken the job at MBH that he was over feeling sorry for himself. Most of the time, he kept that promise. He kept busy, made sure the hunters had what they needed in the way of equipment, intel, and coordination. He made himself indispensable—because if they needed him, he had to be there.

BRIAN

When he'd been at his lowest, before Jamie had come back home and rescued him from himself, he'd considered ending himself. He'd even bought the gun —a Remington handgun that sat in a locked box under his bed. He just hadn't ever bought the bullets.

These days, he rarely thought about offing himself. He was too busy, and some part of him had begun to believe, to hope, that something better was coming. Because he'd lived through the worst a man could face and come out...if not whole, then not completely destroyed.

He had friends who respected him and cared about him, a job he truly enjoyed with new gadgets and tech to keep him from ever being bored. The van, the drones, the advanced surveillance equipment the agency could now afford due to the success of their reality TV show was enabling him to become a bigger part of the operations. He lived for those times, because with the cameras the team wore, he felt as though he was in the thick of the action. He forgot he was chained to a chair. He was with the team, entering that building or clearing. He heard the shouts, the cries, the pops of gunfire. For those fleeting moments, he was fully alive, fully engaged.

So, if he had to spend the occasional morning watching his buddies run around a track while a certain physical therapist gave him pointed glares, so be it. She wasn't going to wear him down. He'd dare her to try.

CHAPTER 2

Raydeen Pickering bit back a smile as she passed the timekeeper on her fifth lap around the high school track. She knew Brian Cobb thought he was doing a good job covering up his emotions as his bounty hunter teammates huffed and puffed their way around the quarter-mile loop, some barely breaking a sweat, others gasping because they'd gotten lazy over the long, cold Montana winter.

They were experiencing a rare snowmelt, temperatures in the low forties, and Raydeen had challenged them all to join her and her usual running buddy, Dylan "Hook" Hoecker, for a Saturday morning sprint. However, everyone, even Brian, knew this was all about him. Sure, she would have enjoyed the extra company anytime, but her focus was on Brian, and as his good friends, the rest of the bounty hunter crew were game to help her keep the pressure on.

BRIAN

On the far end of the track from Brian, his best friend and one of his bosses, Jamie Reynolds, pulled up beside Raydeen. Wisps of Jamie's blonde hair stuck to her red cheeks, but she smiled as she matched her pace to Raydeen's. "He's doing a terrible job of pretending he's not watching you."

Raydeen snorted. "Likely, he's still cussing under his breath. He did not want to join us today."

Jamie's expression grew wistful. "It has to be hard watching all of us, so able-bodied, circling this track. He used to smoke me when we ran for PT in the Army."

"Don't feel sorry for him," Raydeen said, shaking her head. "Brian's mobile. His brain injury isn't holding him back none. If you feel sorry for him, it'll only make it easier for him to make excuses for why he's still sittin' in that chair."

Jamie shot her a sideways glance. "Raydeen, do you think maybe he feels like he's been through enough? That he's satisfied with his present mobility? He gets around fine in his chair. Even plays basketball with the guys."

For a second, Raydeen wondered if her stubborn pursuit of Brian was really for his good or for hers. *Nah.* "If he was satisfied sitting in his chair, he wouldn't hide behind his work. He'd ask a girl out and see about taking care of his manly needs."

Jamie barked a laugh. "His manly needs?"

Raydeen wrinkled her nose. "I'd lay money the

only action that man has had since he lost his legs is what his own hand gives him."

Jamie blew out a breath that filled her cheeks. "He's in a much better state of mind than when I first got back here. You didn't see him then—skinny as a rail, his hair down to his shoulders, and looking so scruffy you just knew he didn't bathe all that often. When I see him now, I see life in his eyes. He's come a long way."

"He has," Raydeen agreed, remembering the man she'd first met at a Soldier's Sanctuary meeting nearly a year ago. He'd come, accompanied by Jamie. Back then, he'd had a feral look, his gaze constantly darting toward the door. She'd attended in her capacity as a physical therapist working with soldiers returning from war with physical disabilities. When she'd introduced herself for the first time to Brian, he'd ghosted her for the rest of the meeting. Once she'd started to work with his teammate, Hook, it hadn't been so easy for him to escape her. "Jamie, if I thought he was happy with his progress, I wouldn't press."

"I know, just..."

Raydeen gave a jerky nod. "Give him time. I know. But he's had time, and my patience is wearin' thin."

Jamie grinned. "So, why don't you ask him out?"

Raydeen turned her head to stare at the woman. "Ask him out? I want to be his therapist."

"I see the way you look at him," the blonde said,

her light brown eyes twinkling. "I also see the way he looks at you..."

Then she sped up, leaving Raydeen behind. Which was fine with her. The very idea. She didn't date her patients. She neared the bleachers where Brian sat, holding out his arm.

"Ten minutes, ten seconds. Get the lead out of your ass, Pickering," he said, giving her a smirk.

"And she thinks I want to date that asshole?" she muttered under her breath once she was well past him. She didn't want to date him. No way. Straddle his lap and sink on his cock? Maybe. She'd noticed the way he looked at her lately, too, when he thought she wasn't looking. His dark eyes smoldering, eating her up. Damn, the bastard had her thinking things she shouldn't. Had her hot and itchy. Not for the first time, she wondered what he'd do if she walked up behind him and bent to lick the rim of his ear. Take a little nibble. Would he shiver or jerk away?

The thought was tempting, but if she tried it and he rejected her, she'd lose any chance of rehabilitating him.

Best to keep things all business. Get him thinking about trying on a pair of prosthetic limbs. There wasn't any reason in the world other than his own stubbornness that was stopping him from getting back more of what he'd lost.

She must have slowed her pace more than she'd thought because Dagger and Hook lapped her.

"Better pick up the pace, Raye," Hook said,

turning to run backwards as he gave her an "eat shit" grin.

"You fall on your ass and break your hook, don't come running to me to get it repaired again," she groused.

He laughed and turned, and then cursed because Dagger had used his inattention to put twenty yards between them.

"Catch him, baby," Hook's girlfriend, Felicity Gronkowski, called out. The little redhead stood and held her fist aloft, pumping the air to encourage him while Quincy's fiancée, Tamara Adams, laughed beside her.

"Why don't you join us?" Hook called out to Felicity.

She raised a foot to show him her heeled boots. "I'm not dressed for it. Plus, I'm getting breathless just watching you guys!"

Beside her, Dagger's girl, Lacey Jones, hooted. "Dagger, baby, don't you let Hook catch you. I've got something for you if you finish first!"

Dagger raised a middle finger. He likely didn't have the breath to holler back at her. His beefy frame wasn't made for speed.

Reaper Stenberg, Brian's other boss, pulled up beside Raydeen, breathing hard. "I'm too old for this shit," he growled.

Raydeen glanced behind her to see whether his wife was still on the track. "Carly's slowin' down. Why don't you go encourage her?" she said slyly, giving him a reason not to try to keep up with the two more energetic bounty hunters.

Reaper gave her a narrow-eyed look. "Good idea." Then he fell back to jog beside the curvy brunette.

Raydeen knew the hunters well—through Hook—but also because she tended to drop in on their office a lot. They didn't seem to mind, likely enjoying the way her presence got under Brian's skin.

Cochise, Animal, and Quincy were the only hunters not on the track that morning. When the crew had arrived, Reaper told her he'd sent them to Colorado to track down a high-dollar skip. However, everyone else was there. Even the hunter's ladies. Animal's girl, Allie Travers, wasn't running. She'd come with her camera to video the team for the agency's website. Although why fans wanted to see the hunters dressed in sweats and beanies, sweating bullets as they ran, was beyond her.

Thinking about all the changes that had come to the office Brian ran—the new hunters, the reality TV show—she was amazed he'd adapted so well. Brian wasn't a fluid, flexible kind of guy, and he didn't like change. He needed control over his environment. Things, and people, in their places. With so many hunters to keep track of now, she knew he had to be a bit stressed. Not that he showed it.

She worried about what he didn't show, and wished he had a confidant, someone to talk to. She wished it could be her.

However, she knew if he ever considered her as more than a friend, she'd still be a distant second to the object of his affections. Raydeen doubted Jamie was even aware that her best friend was in love with her.

Lot of good that would ever do him. Jamie loved her husband Sky. No, Brian needed to open himself up to consider someone else, otherwise he'd be pining for a woman he could never have for the rest of his days.

And that wasn't healthy. She knew. She'd grieved a long time after the loss of her husband. Also Army, like Brian. Also grievously wounded. Only Mike hadn't had the balls to suck it up and get on with his life. Before he'd even left rehab at Walter Reed, he'd hung himself inside his room while she'd left to get a bite to eat at the cafeteria.

Raydeen stretched her legs and raised her arms, speeding up. As her feet pounded the track, she pushed back the memory of arriving to find attendants crowding the doorway of Mike's room. She'd known before she'd pushed her way inside that he was gone. Hell, he'd never really come back from Iraq. What had arrived Stateside had been a husk of the man she'd loved.

So, why was she ready to take on more heartbreak? How could she be attracted to another amputee? She passed Brian without looking at him, keeping her expression fierce as she raced.

What was she doing? He didn't want her help.

He'd made that clear by the way he made her pry him from his office every time she showed up for her workout "dates" with Hook. Hook had figured out quickly what she was trying to do and was all for shaking the other man out of his comfort zone. But she hadn't made much headway.

As she rounded the track again, she dared a glance his way.

Although Dagger and Hook had finished their two miles and were standing beside him, his gaze was locked on her.

Once again, she felt pulled in by the intensity of his dark eyes. The man wasn't immune to this attraction that hummed between them. She felt it. There was no way he didn't as well.

Hell, he'd taken off his jacket and had it laying across his lap. She'd bet anything that she, not Jamie, was the reason.

She slowed her pace, jogging the last hundred yards and lowering her arms. When she got closer, she gave him a steady stare as she closed in, reached for the arms of his wheelchair, and bent over him. "Time?" she asked breathing hard, noting that his gaze went to her heaving chest. No way he wasn't interested in her "girls".

He cleared his throat and raised the stopwatch. "Fifteen-forty-five," he said, his tone curt. "You've done better."

She didn't straighten. Still bent toward him, she curved her lips. "Next time," she whispered. She pushed away and turned, and then slowly walked away, knowing he was watching her ass wag as she left.

At her car, she reached inside her gym bag for a bottle of water, unscrewed the top, and poured it down her throat.

Hook jogged toward her.

She gave him a scowl. "It's not fair you still have energy," she said, mopping the quickly cooling sweat from her forehead with a towel.

Hook waggled his eyebrows. "Whatever you're doing, keep it up. Haven't seen him this...um, agitated, ever."

She snorted. "I knew he had a hard-on."

Hook laughed. "Yeah, well. Guys get 'em. Sometimes, they really do have a mind of their own."

"I understand anatomy, Hook," she said, grimacing. "Thing is, I shouldn't be teasing him. Not if I'm going to work with him."

Hook gave her a pointed stare. "How about you be his *friend*, first. Might get you further."

She gave him the stink-eye and shut her door. "Be sure to call me when you're free for another run."

"Don't worry about dropping in the office, anytime, whether I'm there or not. You don't need an excuse."

He turned and jogged back to his truck. Felicity gave a wave before climbing into the passenger seat.

Raydeen glanced around. Reaper and Carly were

already pulling out of the parking lot. Dagger and Lacey were kissing against the side of his truck.

"Hey, get a room," Brian called out as he wheeled past them. He made a beeline for his van, his head down, likely trying to ignore her presence. Hard to do since she'd parked right beside his vehicle.

She waited while he reached up, opened the driver's door, then placed his hands on the steering wheel and the arm rest on the door to pull himself up into his seat. Then he leaned down for his wheelchair, folded it inward, and lifted it over his body to deposit in the space behind the passenger seat.

Inwardly, she acknowledged that every little aspect of his life was harder than most folks'. She took for granted the fact she could easily slide right inside her car. Everything Brian did as he went about doing "normal" tasks took longer.

She walked over to his window and tapped on it.

The window whirred downward. "Raye, what you need?" he asked, giving her a baleful stare.

She wondered what he'd say if she said, *You*. "I was wondering...." Pausing, she ignored the thumping of her heart. "Would you like to grab breakfast with me?"

He blinked, but his expression didn't change. "I have to get back to the office."

"It's Saturday," she said, trying not to sound like a smart ass. "Even a bounty hunter wrangler deserves a morning off."

"Bounty hunter wrangler?" he said, arching an eyebrow.

"That's what you do, right?" she said, smiling. "Has to be as hard as herdin' cats."

"Ain't that the truth." His mouth twitched. "Guess we could. Bear Lodge Café is wheelchair-friendly. Just one thing..."

She gave him a nod. "Shoot."

"No pressure about the Sanctuary."

"Deal," she said, then reached inside to shake his hand.

She wasn't a little girl, and had never thought of her hands as dainty, but his large hand engulfed hers in heat. When he ended the shake, she felt disappointed. His touch had felt...right. Made her want more. In other places. She pointed toward the front of his vehicle. "Maybe we could ride together...?"

"Sure," he said, his expression shuttering again.

She knew he was already regretting accepting her invitation, and she was just prolonging his exposure by riding with him, but she was beginning to think Hook might be right.

Maybe she ought to pursue him. Be his *friend*. She could make him see that it was time to trade the candle he carried for Jamie for one that could burn just for him. And if she had to do the chasing, so be it. She'd prove to him he was mooning over the wrong woman. Ms. Right was climbing right inside his damn van.

CHAPTER 3

Brian didn't know what the hell had happened, but the soft-voiced, soft-mouthed Raydeen he'd talked to at his window wore a hard smile and a militant gleam in her eye when she climbed into the passenger seat.

Again, he drew deep breaths, trying to hide the fact he was calming himself because his dick was getting hard again, and damn he didn't want her to know she made him that way—far faster than Jamie ever had.

With that calculating glint in her eye, he couldn't stop himself from imagining her nude, rising above him, her full breasts swaying as she straddled him and sank down, engulfing his cock in a single stroke.

And now, his cock pressed hard against his zipper. He bit back a groan.

Her lips slid into a grin. "Change your mind, Brian?"

Was he only imagining that her voice had dropped an octave? "Course not. Breakfast. Everyone eats it. Or should." Fuck, he sounded like an idiot. He cleared his throat and put the vehicle into reverse. Using the spinner knob on the steering wheel, which made it possible for him to steer with one hand while his left worked the gas and brake lever, he backed out the van then drove smoothly forward, entering the school drive before turning onto the highway that led into town.

"That was fun today," she said, her gaze on the road ahead. "Who won, anyway? Dagger or Hook?"

One side of Brian's mouth quirked upward. "Dagger, but only by a nose."

"And only because Hook gave him the advantage running backwards like that." She leaned against the passenger door and angled her body towards his. "What did they wager anyway?"

"Their dignity," Brian said, his smile stretching. "The loser has to film a vlog with Lacey while she tests a new mask. It's pink and sparkles."

Raydeen's smile stretched her lush mouth, showing most of her white teeth. Her mouth was his second favorite feature. Not that he ought to have favorites. No, it was stupid to notice the light brown freckles on her cheeks and nose, but they made her seem more approachable. Less intimidating. At least, when her dark eyebrows weren't lowered into her "Amazon-fierce" frown. He remembered how she'd looked that last lap, her dark, corkscrew curls floating around her head, her long, sturdy legs stretching, her breasts swaying...

Jesus-fucking-Christ. If she looked at his lap now...

He drew another deep breath and let it out slowly. So, she was attractive. In a scary way. No, scary wasn't the right word, because he didn't really live in fear of Raydeen, although he ought to. She represented everything he'd fled after weeks of rehab. Another bull-nosed therapist, who thought she knew better than he did about what he should want. Though to be fair, she hadn't brought up the subject of prosthetics in a really long time.

Still, she was in his van. That might just mean she was getting sneakier about how she was going to convince him that standing tall should be the end-all goal of all double amputees.

She couldn't be inside his van because she was really interested in him.

"I like the haircut," she said, then turned to stare out the window again.

He shot her a glance. Her dusky cheeks were pink. Was she embarrassed about giving him a compliment? "Thanks," he mumbled. He'd cut his hair short purely for convenience. Less to wash. Short enough he wouldn't need to get another cut for months.

"I enjoyed having a look inside your new ops van that day."

A subject he could warm up to... Now, he knew

she was fishing for something. "You should see it when the team's on a mission—all the monitors lit."

"You said you can operate the drone from the console, too...?"

"Yeah, with a joystick. Although when the team's on the ground and I'm operating the stick, I really need another operator in the van with me. Felicity has gone out with me a time or two, but we're going to have to train up someone else, someone who works for the agency fulltime. Felicity is pretty busy with her own day job."

"We?"

He gave her a questioning glance.

"You said, '*We're* going to have to train up someone else...'"

He grimaced. "Well, me. I'll have to train someone."

From the corner of his eye, he watched as she studied him. "Bet you don't like having someone else in your space."

"I don't like or dislike..." He frowned, because he knew that was lie. "It's not about me, Raye, it's about what the team needs—eyes in the air and on the ground."

"Huh." Her lips pursed.

Heat shot straight through him, warming his face and other regions best not contemplated. Because he was pissed with her answer. She didn't believe he was putting the team's needs first. He wasn't getting

BRIAN

warm because her lips looked as though they'd feel like cushions if he kissed them...

Thankfully, the highway had ended and Main Street stretched out in front of them. He drove to the café and parked at the side in a handicapped space. Due to his agitation, he took longer than usual wrestling with his wheelchair to pull it from behind the passenger seat.

"Do you need help?"

"No."

She raised her eyebrows. "How about I go get us a table?"

"Fine."

When she left, he lifted his chair and banged it down, not that the temper tantrum helped. Or had it? His cock wasn't going to embarrass him now.

When he rolled toward the entrance, Raydeen stood holding open the door.

"I know you can open your own doors," she said, giving him a snide grin. "I just like opening my own."

The hint of attitude in her features went a long way toward quenching his embarrassment. He'd pissed her off. She'd pissed him off. He figured they were even now.

"The waitress is getting our table ready," she said, as she followed him inside. "To the right."

Most of the seating was bench-style booths, but toward the rear were small round tables. A waitress was busy pulling away unneeded chairs and gave them a smile as they approached. "I'll get your menus."

"No need," Brian bit out.

"I know what I want," Raydeen said at the same time.

Raising her eyebrows at their terse words, the waitress reached into her apron for her pad. "Well, then, what can I get for you two?"

They placed their orders for the "family-style" plate that featured bacon and ham, two eggs, a small stack of pancakes, and an order of hash browns.

When he glanced at Raydeen after she'd made her order, she wrinkled her nose. "I like to eat. Sue me."

"I wasn't going to say anything. I think..." Again, he raked his glance over her sturdy frame. "I think you shouldn't worry about calories."

"Hmm." She narrowed her eyes. "Is that because you think I'm fat and don't care?"

"You're not fat."

"I'm not a stick-girl."

"No, you're not. You're...built..." Shit, why was he even going there?

"No, finish the thought."

He cleared his throat then nearly choked. Bless her, the waitress arrived with coffees and water. He took a swig of water, hoping the delay would prevent his having to finish.

However, the way Raydeen sat back in her chair, her arms crossed just beneath her breasts, told him that she was going to out-wait him. He sighed. "You're built like a fucking Amazon. Strong, sleek. Powerful."

"You think I'm sleek?" she asked, tilting her head.

"Like a powerful leopard." He was beginning to sweat, because she still didn't look satisfied with his answer, and he was beginning to feel like dork, because he couldn't tell her the truth. Or could he? "Leopards are sturdy, muscled. And yet, when they move, they're graceful in a...full-bodied...sort of way." Yeah, his face was hot. No hiding the fact.

The corners of her mouth twitched. Then she gave a laugh and slapped the table. "Your face!" She laughed some more then bent at the waist. "So, I'm a...a l-leopard?" She pointed at him and snickered.

Brian blew hard, billowing out his cheeks. "You did that on purpose."

"Sure did. Wondered where you'd go, but... damn!" She continued to giggle then chortle, but by then, he didn't care, because he'd never seen this side of Raydeen, her eyes narrowed by laughter, her mouth stretched wide. There were tears in her eyes she laughed so hard.

A wry smile tugged at his mouth. "Glad I could entertain you," he muttered.

She wiped at her tears then sniffed and straightened. "Sorry about that. You're always so serious, so uptight—when I'm around, anyway. Seeing you scramblin' to explain yourself..." Her shoulders shook, but she pretended to zip her mouth. "I'll stop. Right now."

"Please. Everyone's staring." He didn't know that because he couldn't look away from her. He'd always thought her body was hot, but her smiling...? He felt warm again, but not from embarrassment. He felt strangely...happy.

The waitress returned with a large tray, which she set on the table next to theirs, then began setting dishes in front of them.

"Hope you don't have to be anywhere for a while," Raydeen said, waggling her eyebrows. "It's gonna take a while to finish all this."

He unfolded a paper napkin and placed it on his lap. "Didn't you order the biggest plate so we'd have plenty of time together? I know I did."

And that shut her right up.

RAYDEEN SAT STUNNED, her eyebrows shooting upward. He'd delivered that line in a low voice, deeper than before. She'd felt it whisper right across her skin, prickling the surface with goose bumps. Indeed, she had ordered the largest plate because she intended to dawdle and make the most of this opportunity of having him all to herself. She was floored that he'd admitted to doing the same damn thing.

She picked up a piece of bacon, contemplating what to say next, but then sighed. "Bacon's the best, its own dang food group, far as I'm concerned."

BRIAN

"I'm with you," he said. "The first time my parents took me to a breakfast buffet, they said I could eat whatever I wanted. I asked if I could have all the bacon I wanted, and they said yes. When I piled my plate high—with just bacon—they laughed so hard." He waggled his eyebrows back at her and took a bite of his bacon. "I've been an addict all my life."

"Bacon makes everything better," she said with a nod. "See? We have something in common."

They ate in companionable silence for a few minutes. From time to time, she'd glance up from her plate to find him looking at her. On the fourth time, she said, "What? Do I have food on my face?"

He raised a finger and pointed at the right side of her mouth. "A little egg."

"Ooh." She picked up her napkin and dabbed at her mouth, but the paper came back clean. "My mouth was clean. Admit it. You were looking at me."

His gaze went to his plate, and he quickly raised his fork to place potatoes in his mouth. He made a noise as he chewed, pointing at his mouth now.

Raydeen shook her head. "Coward. I know you can't get enough looking at these," she said, plumping up her breasts with her hands. The tee she wore was tight, and he'd probably been staring at the twin points that pressed against the fabric.

Color surged into his cheeks again. "Sorry about that," he said. "Didn't mean to make you uncomfortable."

Raydeen leaned across the table. Leaning over gave him a little glimpse of her cleavage, which she didn't mind sharing. "Do I look uncomfortable, Brian Cobb?" she whispered.

His gaze narrowed. "Are you always this...flirty?"

"How long have you known me? Have you ever seen me flirt with any other man?" She tipped her chin. "Think about that—and be glad you have a napkin coverin' your lap."

The waitress returned to refill their coffees. Her gaze went from Raydeen to Brian and back, and she blinked.

Raydeen could almost hear her inner monologue. *Too bad he doesn't have legs because he's really cute.* Raydeen signaled for the waitress to lean toward her, then cupped the woman's ear and whispered. "His big dick's not gone."

The waitress gasped and backed away, her fleshy bottom hitting the table behind her before she scurried toward the other side of the restaurant.

Raydeen glanced at Brian, hoping he hadn't heard what she'd said. When she got mad, she found it hard to curb her tongue.

He was studying her face.

She bit her bottom lip then blurted, "I told her she had toilet paper on her shoe."

"No, you didn't."

Shit. "Then what did I say?" She raised her chin, challenging him to repeat her words.

"I don't need you defending me."

"No, you don't. You don't need defending."

His gaze remained steady, pinning her to her chair. "Then why did you do it?"

"Because she can't look beyond your wheelchair to the man," Raydeen said, her voice tightening.

He gave her a nod. "Well, then, thank you, but I wonder how you know it's big."

Raydeen sat back. She hadn't known. But now that she did...? "Guess I was just bein' hopeful."

Brian sat still for a moment, his expression not giving away a thing. But then he pressed his lips together, and his shoulders started to shake.

Raydeen threw her napkin on the table. "Don't you laugh at me."

His laughter rang out, and she had to admit it was a beautiful sound. Something she hadn't heard before. Settling back in her chair, she smiled across at him. *Baby, I have your number now. Don't think I won't call it.*

CHAPTER 4

Monday morning, Brian found himself whistling as he placed a fresh filter in the coffee maker and added two full scoops of coffee before sliding the funnel beneath the dispenser. The hunters liked their coffee strong enough to stand a spoon inside a cup. So did he.

He heard a choking sound and jerked his head around to find Jamie standing in the doorway, her eyes wide.

"What?"

She pressed her lips together before replying, "Were you whistling 'Don't Worry, Be Happy'?"

Brian frowned. Had he been? His mind had been elsewhere. "I can't carry a tune. I thought I was whistling 'Down with the Sickness'," he said grumpily.

"You were not," she said, grinning now as she

drew closer. She cleared her throat. "Heard you had a date," she said, her tone sly.

"What date?" he said, although he was pretty sure he knew what she was referring to.

"You and Raydeen. Allie saw you and Raydeen leaving the track together."

Damn busybodies. Didn't this crew have better things to do than gossip? "Well, it wasn't a date. It was...breakfast." Where Raydeen had teased him into a hard-on, and then told the waitress he had a big dick. Thank God, none of them had been inside the café.

"Huh," Jamie said, her eyes narrowing while her smile widened. "Tamara was getting coffee and takeout at the Bear Lodge Café. Said the waitress was all flustered. You know Tamara was a hairdresser, right? She can wring gossip out of a stone..."

His cheeks heated. "Must have been some conversation."

"She said something about Raydeen oversharing about some man's *attributes*..." she said with a waggle of her eyebrows.

"Then you know she wasn't talking about me. Raydeen doesn't know a thing about my...attributes," he muttered.

"Huh." She gave him a wink. "That's okay. You can keep your secrets. Just know this—I think you two look cute together."

Brian scowled, which only set Jamie giggling. Then Tamara stepped through the door. The pink streak in her hair wasn't its usual soft, cotton-candy—it was nearly neon. Brian held up a hand and gave an exaggerated wince.

"Oh, no. You do not get to change the subject," Tamara said, wagging a finger at him. "Spill! I've been dying to hear what happened on your date."

"It wasn't a date," he repeated.

"It was breakfast," Jamie finished for him.

"Pfft," Tamara said, putting a hand on her hip. "Well, it was a steaming-hot breakfast, from what I heard."

"Well, you heard wrong."

Tamara pressed her lips together, her eyes narrowing. Then she shook her head. "Nope, I'm not letting you get away with that. Come on, spill."

Brian glanced at the ceiling. "Seriously, Tam. Do you think someone who looks like Raye—"

"Wait a second, mister," Jamie said, giving him a glare. "Don't you dare finish that statement."

Tamara nodded. "We've all seen the way you two look at each other."

He threw up his hands. "Why does everyone keep saying that? The only reason she's looking at me is because she's measuring me for prosthetics."

"That's not even what she does," Tamara said. "You'd go to a...a guy for that—she just helps you learn to walk on 'em."

Jamie let out a deep breath. "Will you give yourself a break, Brian? Why wouldn't she be interested in you. You're a handsome man, intelligent, a great friend..." When he gave her a baleful look and deliberately glanced down at his legs, she frowned. "Don't you think Raydeen, of all people, would know exactly what she'd be getting herself into?"

He didn't answer, frowning because he didn't want to have this conversation.

Jamie gave him an equally dark scowl right back. "If she's having breakfast with you—and apparently flirting with you—she's interested."

"Well, she can just get *un*-interested. I don't have time to date. We have skips to chase, a production crew about to descend... She'll just have to find someone else to—" He gave Jamie a glare. "She wasn't flirting. She was defending me."

Jamie bugged her eyes. "How on earth was she defending you when she said you have a big dick?"

"For the love of G—"

"What I heard," Tamara said, "was that you two were both eating each other up with your eyes."

"That doesn't even sound anatomically possible," he said, his voice rising with his growing frustration.

"Dude," came a deep voice from the doorway. Reaper strode inside, one eyebrow arched. "If Raydeen is into you, why the hell are you fighting it? She's *hawt*."

"Who's hot?" said Carly, walking in behind him and giving her husband a blistering stare.

"Baby, Raydeen. She was talking about Brian's dick. Said he had a—"

"Ah, heard about that," she said, a smile replacing her frown. "I was over at the café last night—"

Brian opened his mouth to utter another denial, but the three women and Reaper continued to share their "intel"—obviously not needing his input, because when he wheeled right past them, they didn't appear to notice.

When he was back in the bullpen, settled in front of his monitor, he took a deep breath. The sound of laughter from the kitchen spilled into the room but was distant enough for him to ignore. He powered up his monitor and hit the icon to open the agency's daily list.

The tone that rang when the front door opened chimed, and he glanced up to see Dagger and Lacey entering. Lacey's gaze widened when she saw him. "So, I want the skinny on your date!"

Two hours later, after the hunters had their marching orders for the day and had exited the building, Brian sat staring at the screen, not really registering what he was looking at. The silence was deafening.

While the hunters had all been there, Hook arriving late because he'd waited for Felicity to return home after a late-night surveillance mission, Brian had been the center of their attention. A weird experience for him. They liked to gossip, and he'd never given them anything juicy to ruminate over.

For all his protestations, he realized he'd kind of liked being hazed. He'd felt like one of them, because they'd been just as single-minded going after the "deets" of his breakfast with Raydeen as they'd ever been dissecting their own relationships.

Not that he'd given them much to mull over. "Just the facts, Jack," Carly had muttered, following the women out of the kitchen to filter into the bullpen. "So, if you won't tell us what you discussed, tell us about her. Tell us what you learned about Raydeen."

He'd shrugged. "What do you mean? We didn't go into our life histories or anything."

"But what did you two talk about?"

He made a growling noise, but knew he'd have to give them something or they'd never leave him alone. "She said she ordered the biggest breakfast plate because she intended to take her time finishing, seeing as she had me all to herself."

The women smiled.

Reaper, again, arched a single eyebrow. "So, she likes her bacon."

"Something she said we have in common," Brian said, feeling vindicated. It was all about the bacon. Then he closed his mouth because he hadn't intended to reveal any more details.

Carly plopped down in a desk chair and scooted it closer. Jamie sat on the edge of the table that held his monitor. Tamara sat and leaned an elbow on the tabletop then settled her chin on top of her hand.

"Well, don't leave them hanging?" Reaper growled.

His cheeks began to burn. "Um, she kept insisting that she was making me uncomfortable."

"As uncomfortable as you were at the track?" Jamie asked, chuckling.

When he didn't answer, Tamara rolled her eyes. "Jesus, we all know you got hard watching her run."

"He did?" Reaper said, glancing around the group.

"I guess guys don't check out each other's dicks," Tamara said.

"And you women do?" Reaper said, sounding horrified.

"We notice your...packages..." Jamie said, "just like you check out our boobs."

Reaper gave a huff. "We do n—"

"Actually, she accused me of ogling hers," Brian said, then shook his head, instantly regretting opening his big mouth again. He'd only said it because Reaper had been so adamant that he didn't do that, but Brian knew it was a lie. Half the time he talked to Carly he was staring at her chest. "Um, she said I couldn't get enough of looking at these," he said, cupping his hands and holding them under his chest as he mimicked Raydeen hefting her beautiful tits.

"And she'd be right, yeah?" Tamara said, grinning.

Brian rolled his eyes. "I'm pleading the fifth."

BRIAN

"What else did you talk about?" Jamie asked, her voice softer now.

"Uh, Amazons and leopards..." He pulled at the neck of his shirt. "I need to fix that thermostat. It's getting hot in here."

"That's because there are too many bodies in this kitchen jaw-jacking instead of working!" Hook said from the entrance.

When had the door chime sounded?

"Yeah, we got work to do," Reaper said, nodding and looking relieved by the change of subject.

Hook had given Brian a wink, and then clapped him on the shoulders with both hands. "So, what do you have that could pay for the new living room suite Felicity is keen on buying?"

He owed Hook a huge one for pulling him out of the breach. Who knew women could be so ruthlessly persistent when it came to romance?

Not that romance had had a thing to do with his and Raydeen's "date."

Fuck. Now, he was thinking the word, too. He snorted. *As if.* Someone like Raydeen would never in a million years be interested in someone like him. She deserved a full-bodied man. Someone who could keep up with her. Bend her over an arm for a deep kiss...or a couch...

Jesus, just the thought of seeing her like that made him want things he was better off never imagining.

Again, he snorted. Since he'd met the woman, he

41

hadn't been able to control where his imagination led. At times, he saw her as a drill instructor, a metal whistle between her lips as she ran alongside him, telling him to wheel faster and faster. Sometimes, he wondered whether she ever wore a dress or something...pink. Something soft and feminine that floated around her tawny legs as she walked ahead of him. Most times, though, he imagined what she'd look like first thing in the morning as she turned her head on his pillow.

Funny, he'd never imagined Jamie in his bed...

The door chimed again, and he blew out an exasperated breath, sure one of the women had "forgotten" something, just to provide an excuse to return and badger him some more. When he turned toward the door, his heart thudded in his chest.

Oh, dude, you've got it bad...

RAYDEEN PUSHED through the door and drew a deep breath. The parking lot out front was empty, so she knew the other hunters had already left. Brian would know straight away she was here to see him. Good thing she had an excuse.

When his glance turned toward her, his features went still. His face, anyway. Not his eyes. Again, she saw heat banked in his dark eyes before he blinked and gave her a nod.

"Mornin'. What brings you here today?"

To her ears, his voice held a note of tension. She

held up a box of doughnuts. "I brought breakfast," she said, forcing a smile and hoping she didn't look too eager.

"The crew's already out on the road."

She arched a brow. The box wasn't that big. "I brought you some of Gladys's at Bear Lodge Bakery's famous maple bars."

"Oh." He cleared his throat. "Coffee's been on the burner for a while. I could make a fresh pot."

"I had a cup already. Too many and I get the shakes," she said, holding up a hand and shaking it.

"Um, you can put the box here," he said, patting the table beside him.

She moved closer, knowing she was acting a little squirrely, not feeling her usual confidence. Why the hell was she here? Oh yeah, she had a favor to ask...

Setting the box on the table, she pondered how to broach her request.

"Raydeen..." he said, peering at her face. "Again, why are you here?"

He didn't sound irritated, which was a good thing. In fact, his voice was softer...no, hoarser. A sound she could get used to, she thought. "I, uh, need a favor."

His brows furrowed. "You need me to do something for you?"

"I don't know who else to ask..."

"Just shoot. I won't know whether I can help if you don't tell me."

"Okay," she drew in a deep breath. "There's this

guy..."

His expression shuttered, and she realized maybe he was reading more into that than she intended. "He's a patient."

"Okay...?"

"He hasn't shown up for therapy in two weeks."

"You try calling him?"

"I did. And I dropped by the address he listed when he began therapy with me, but his landlord said he'd moved out a month ago."

"Why are you so concerned about him, Raye? Maybe he moved or decided to be with family..."

"Brian, he never missed an appointment, and he showed up to work out in the Sanctuary's gym nearly every day. He wouldn't have quit without telling someone...without telling me."

"He's important to you?"

She shrugged. "As important as any patient I work with."

His eyebrows lowered. "You show up at his work with donuts, too?"

Raydeen snorted through her nose. "I've only brought you maple bars, Brian, and I've never defended the size of anyone else's dick."

Brian gave her a long look. "Okay, so you want me to dig around to figure out what happened to him? Is there something that worries you about him in particular?"

Raydeen grimaced. "He has a problem with OxyContin. The VA quit dispensing. Some of the guys, they found another source. I don't know much, but I think it's not completely legal."

"And you didn't think to report it to anyone?"

"I reported my suspicions to my supervisor. What he did with that information, I have no clue."

"And you think there might be a connection to the drugs and his going missing?"

"No." She shrugged. "Maybe, but you asked me about why I was worried. Kenan always had a positive attitude. He worked hard to learn to use his prosthetic, but he needed help with his phantom pain. Sometimes, it was just too much." Her shoulders sank, unsure what Brian could do if Kenan had decided he didn't want to be found. And if Brian did find him, whether he'd be willing to accept her help. Still, she felt it was her duty to do what she could. She'd failed once. She wouldn't again.

Seeing her concern, Brian nodded. Phantom pain was something he could relate to. Only, he'd decided to deal with the pain. It was the price he paid for living when Benny had died.

"I'll help you. Might be a little harder, seeing as my usual resources might be reluctant to help, since he doesn't have an outstanding warrant..."

"Whatever you can do..."

"Okay, then." He pushed a pad of paper across the desk toward her. "Write down everything you know..."

CHAPTER 5

After Raydeen provided everything she knew about Kenan, Brian told her she could take off. He'd make some calls and see where they led before he spoke to her again. She'd huffed a breath, but he'd held firm. He'd call when he had something.

No way could he have worked with her underfoot, so to speak. Already, the light scent of her perfume lingered. Flowers and spice. Which flowers and spices, he had no clue, but he liked the scent. Smelled...sexy. He tried to ignore her essence as he rolled back to his desk. Raydeen had worn a sweater that hugged her tits just right, and she'd given him a nice view of the profile of her breasts, large but firm. Every time she'd turned. Her bra must not have been lined because he'd seen a hint of tip. The pretty green sweater had been cropped and fell to the waist of her jeans, which meant every time she'd reached or bent, he'd gotten a nice slice of her firm belly. And those jeans...? He couldn't think of the way they'd made her ass look, like she'd been poured into them, a sweet upside-down heart of a bottom that looked just as softly cushioned as her full lips, to say nothing of the long length of her legs tucked into scarred, heeled cowboy boots.

Fuck me... He grimaced while he readjusted his thickening cock. Now, he wished he could get right on the search for Kenan Reynolds so he could call her, and maybe talk her into having dinner while they discussed what he'd learned...

Only, he had real work to get out of the way first —payroll to complete and calls to make for the team. Payroll didn't take any time at all, because he'd already spent days deciphering the team's expense reports. All he had to do was list any sick time—there was none—any vacation—again, none—and then let the program do the magic. The hunters earned commissions, which he paid upon receipt of the bail bondsmen's checks, but they also earned a small salary to tide them over between commissions. Since they'd moved from checks to automatic deposits, paying everyone was a breeze.

Then he moved onto the cold calls he made to run down leads for the hunters. Something he was getting good at—lying to strangers to ingratiate himself or put the fear of God into them in order to gain their cooperation.

Dagger and Lacey were shaking down friends of a kid who'd been busted dealing drugs to middle schoolers, so he spoke with teachers, coaches, even a pastor, until he discovered that Austin Sommers had spent time at a friend's cabin the previous summer. He texted the location to the couple then moved onto calls to strip clubs in Bozeman where he located the girlfriend of a ranch hand who had rustled cattle on some celebrity's ranch near Flathead Lake. That information he passed along to Reaper and Carly.

"She goes by Sparkle Plenty," Brian said, his tone dry, "and she won't be onstage until after six."

"Another titty bar?" Carly said, sounding disgusted.

Reaper chuckled in the background. "I wonder if the 'Plenty' means she has big tits or a big a—*oomph!* Why'd you do that? I only said what we both were wondering."

"I was not wondering..." she said, with a deadly edge to her voice.

"You two have fun," Brian said, grinning as he ended the call.

At last, he had time to turn his attention to Raydeen's request.

He glanced through the copy of Kenan Reynold's Soldiers' Sanctuary intake form. He began by calling the number the veteran had given for his next of kin —one Dewey Reynolds, his father.

"Hello," a man answered on the fifth ring.

"Is this Dewey Reynolds?"

"Who's askin'?" the man said, his words sharpening.

Given the hint of suspicion in the older man's voice, he decided to lie as close to the truth as he could manage. "I know Kenan from the Soldier's Sanctuary. I was hoping you'd know where he is. I tried his place, but his landlord said he moved out. I'm worried about him."

There was a long pause. "You a friend?"

"Yeah," he said, his voice roughening, because he really didn't like lying. "Name's Brian. I'm an amputee, too."

"Army, like Kenan?"

"Reserves, yeah. I was an MP."

The man sighed. "I don't know where he is, but I'm worried. It's not like him not to call at least once a week, and I haven't heard from him in two."

"Well, damn. I was hoping he'd at least touched base with family."

"I've tried most of his friends from the VFW, but they haven't seen him either. I was getting ready to call the police and report him as missing, but I didn't want to cause him any trouble if he's just wanting to spend some time alone. He's had enough of trouble."

"I only know him through Soldiers' Sanctuary, but does he have any old friends, maybe from before he was in the Army, that I might talk to? He's been missing meetings and therapy sessions. I worry about where his head is..."

"Kenan has an old friend from high school, Daryl

Walker. These days, he's bad news. If Kenan's talking to Daryl, it can't be good. But that's the only person I can think of."

"Well, sir, thank you for talking to me. I'll let you know if I find anything out."

"You do that. And take care, son."

Brian rang off and sat for a minute, thinking about the fact Kenan had a dad who cared about him, and that he'd kept in touch with. He glanced through the notes on the sheet but didn't find any other name that might lead him to another contact, so he conducted an online search for Daryl Walker.

As it turned out, Kenan's father was correct. Walker was bad news. He'd bonded out of jail three times and done an eighteen-month stint in prison. Every bust had been drug-related, ranging from possession of cocaine to the final charge of distribution of methamphetamines and marijuana. The last time had been two months ago, and his address was listed.

The phone rang. "Montana Bounty Hunters, you've got Brian."

"Not yet, I don't."

Brian bit back a groan. "Hi there, Rosalie," he greeted the *Bounty Hunters of the Northwest* film crew's director.

"Just wanted to touch base and make sure you and your team will be ready for us next week. We'll be arriving in Bear Lodge bright and early on Monday."

BRIAN

Gritting his teeth, he muttered, "Forewarned is—"

"Don't say it like that, Bri," Rosalie said in her too perky voice. "Remember, we'll be spending some time with you this season, too."

Brian shook his head, even though he had agreed to being shadowed when Rosalie had backed him into a corner, literally, at the wrap party the previous fall. He'd hoped she'd been too drunk to remember.

"This season we really want to get up close and personal with the team. See inside their homes, their relationships. Got a girlfriend, Bri?"

"Uh..." His mind shot straight to Raydeen.

"You and Raydeen finally hook up?"

His eyebrows shot up. *What?* "We—"

"Let her know we'll need to get some releases signed. Gotta go!"

Brian stared at the phone in his hand. His stomach was starting to hurt. He wondered if he could talk Raydeen into being his girlfriend for the shoot, just so he didn't have to spend as much time being the main focus of the "Brian" segment.

His phone rang again. This time, he checked to see who was calling before he answered. The screen read *Raydeen*.

His heart pumped a little faster. "Hey, I was just about to call you."

"You found something?"

"I did. Spoke to his dad first."

"I talked to his dad, too. It was a complete bust."

"Well, he gave me a name. An old high school buddy of Kenan's, Daryl Walker. He's been in and out of jail on drug charges. Seeing as you're concerned Kenan might have been looking for Oxy, Daryl seems like a legitimate lead."

"Give me his address. I'll head over to his place."

"You will not," Brian said, his tone firm. "He's a drug dealer. What are you going to do? Knock on his front door and ask him if he's been dealing Oxy to Kenan?"

"No, but I could tell him I'm a friend and ask whether he's seen him."

"And he's going to want to know how you got his name. What are you going to say then?"

Raydeen was quiet for a moment. "Well, what the hell else can I do?"

Brian blew out a breath that filled his cheeks. "How about we stake out his place and figure out who Daryl Walker is, see who visits him?"

"What about Kenan?"

"I have some toys. We could listen in to see if he mentions Kenan."

"A stakeout, huh?"

Maybe she snorted, but there was no hiding the hint of intrigue in her voice.

"Where are you right now?"

"Home."

"Give me forty minutes, and I'll pick you up."

"Got something to write with? I'll give you the address."

"I know where you live, Raydeen." He wasn't proud of the fact he'd looked her up a while ago, but he'd been curious about Raydeen Pickering and had wanted to be sure she was on the up and up. After all, she was in and out of the agency, worked closely with Hook—it was just due diligence to check her out. *Right.*

Forty minutes later, Raydeen climbed into the sleek black ops van. "This cool with your bosses?"

Using the spinner knob on the steering wheel and the hand control lever for the gas and brake, Brian expertly backed out of the parking space and drove out of the apartment parking lot. "Jamie and Reaper will be glad I'm blowing the carbon out of the engine."

She arched an eyebrow.

He grimaced. "Okay, so maybe they wouldn't like me doing surveillance on a drug dealer, but they'd have no issue with me using the van. They want me to practice with the gadgets."

"I don't want to get you into any trouble."

"It's not like they'd fire me. If they knew what I was doing, sure they'd be worried." He gave a careless shrug. "But it's not like I don't know how to run an op."

"You do, right?"

"Of course. I mean, I'm not the one making the decisions on the ground, but I do direct action based on what I can see that they can't. I know how to surveil a target."

"And they won't mind you being out of the office?"

"They'd be singing glory halleluiahs that I'm out and about. Jamie's always telling me I need to get out of that building more. Besides, this van is wired. I can access the server via satellite if they need anything."

Her lips pursed then stretched into a small grin. "This is kind of exciting."

He wrinkled his nose. "Tell me that an hour from now. Stakeouts are boring."

"Good thing I brought snacks," she said, patting her backpack.

"Oh? What'd you bring?"

Her smile deepened. "You miss lunch?"

"Yeah, and it's close to dinner. I haven't had anything since those maple bars."

"Well, as soon as we arrive at our destination, I'll show you what I've got," she said, waggling her eyebrows.

Brian laughed. "Not going to go there..."

DARYL WALKER's house was a ratty cracker box with, thankfully, an overgrown yard. Or so Brian murmured under his breath as he parked the van next to the curb two houses down from Daryl's.

"Why's that a good thing?" she asked, curious about how this would work.

"Because someone has to sneak up to the house and plant this against the wall," he said, reaching behind him and pulling something from a black canvas bag. When he held up his hand, what looked like a thick disk with a wire attached to it sat in the center of his palm.

"And that someone would be...?" But she was only teasing. Sneaking through weeds and bushes wasn't in Brian's wheelhouse.

"Only if you're comfortable doing it," he said. "Seriously. If we want to listen inside the house, this wireless wall microphone has to be against the siding." Glancing at the house, he continued, "I'm guessing there's not much insulation between the siding and the drywall, because it's likely broken down over the years, and it doesn't look like they take care of the place. We could get a really good signal."

She plucked up the disk. One side was sticky. "And you have the receiver where?"

He hooked a thumb over his shoulder. Behind the two seats and through the dark, black-out curtains stretched a row of monitors and other equipment atop a workbench table on one side, a deep storage bench on the opposite, plus a couple of folding chairs, stuck to the wall with Velcro. She knew because she'd been there before, admiring his "rig" when it had been his latest toy.

"Goody," she said. "We can eat at the workbench."

"Let's watch for a few, first. Make sure there's no

movement outside before you sneak closer. And I need to run the plates on the car in the drive. Just to make sure it's his."

The sun was dipping below the horizon, and the shadows stretched. She watched the house, feeling a little nervous but also strangely excited to be here with Brian. She knew this wasn't his usual thing. If he surveilled, it was to watch the feed from numerous cameras his teammates wore on helmets or had installed in trees or corners or from one of the drones he operated from inside the van. That last bit blew her mind. He'd shown her a taped recording of one hunt through a national forest where the team had been pinned down by a shooter. Brian had been able to direct the team to safely approach the shooter's location using his "bird's eye" view.

Brian turned his seat then moved from it to his wheelchair, which was just behind the driver's seat. Then he wheeled into the back of the van. "We don't have to watch the house through the windows. Let me get the monitors fired up."

For the moment, Raydeen kept her gaze on the house, thinking it might be kind of funny if no one was inside and they wasted hours surveilling an empty house.

Hours. Alone with Brian. Brian of the bedroom eyes. Brian with the lost boy look married to his rugged features. There were so many secrets she wanted to know, like whether he preferred fucking missionary or while being ridden cowgirl style. If the house was empty, she wondered if they could make this "date" deliver in another way...

CHAPTER 6

After Brian fired up the computers, captured the satellite signal, and homed the cameras installed on the van on Dylan Walker's house, he turned to Raydeen who sat watching through the window. With her face in profile, her gaze turned away, he had a moment to enjoy the view.

He liked seeing her in profile for more than admiring the curve of her pretty tits. Her nose was a little long and tipped upward. Her cheeks were prominent with hollows beneath them. Golden-brown freckles dappled her cheeks and nose, and he wanted to lick every last one of them.

They might have hours and hours alone inside this van. *Soooo*, of course, his mind went straight to blow jobs.

And, of course, she turned to look at him at precisely that moment. He wasn't sure what his expression betrayed, but she licked slowly around her lips before smiling.

"We're all set," he said, then cleared his throat because his voice came out hoarse.

She reached toward her feet for the backpack. "And now, I can feed you."

Her own voice was a little husky, which intrigued him. Or maybe she was just catching a cold.

He maneuvered his chair around to move farther down the table. The cameras captured a view of the front of the house and along part of the side.

"How long we gotta watch before I go stick that thing on his ratty siding?"

"When we finish eating...?" he responded, not looking at her now because he was doing his best to will his cock into taking a rest.

"I didn't bring a meal so much as finger foods. I do like to nibble."

He opened his mouth to say something smart, but what he wanted nibbled stole away his words, so he clamped his lips shut.

She gave a husky laugh, and he turned his head toward her. Her eyes were filled with mischief.

"You know exactly what you're doing to me, don't you?" he grumbled.

"Your man-o-meter is registering your pulse," she said, gazing pointedly at his crotch. "I like taking a reading now and then."

"Raye..."

She pushed up from her captain's chair and walked toward him, and then abruptly turned toward a folding chair and ripped it off the Velcro. "Love that sound. Makes me itchy." Opening the chair, she faced it backward and straddled it, her legs opening over the seat.

Which naturally drew his gaze and made him think about her making that move over his lap...when his pants were down and his cock pointing toward the ceiling. "You're a tease."

"I don't tease, baby," she said, lowering her voice. "I promise. Now, let me feed you."

Flipping open her backpack, she withdrew what looked like a Japanese bento box, and began opening the layers of trays. Inside were vegetables and fruit, all in bite-sized portions, a cup of hummus and another of some white cream, which she dipped a strawberry in then lifted it to her mouth. Her lips wrapped around the juicy fruit, and she bit. Her eyes rolled back and closed, and a deep moan slipped free.

He couldn't help it. He laughed.

She opened one eye. "Too much?"

"Not enough," he said, lifting another strawberry, swiping it into the cream then holding it up for her to take from his fingers. Where he got the nerve, he wasn't sure, but the look in her eyes was encouraging.

She leaned forward and opened wide. He placed it on her tongue, but she moved her head forward and closed her lips around his fingers, drawing off them slowly and taking the fruit.

After she swallowed it, she glanced from his wheelchair to the table. "Will it hold your weight?"

He swallowed hard. Jesus, was he dreaming? "And yours...but... I haven't done this in a really long time, and I'm not losing my pants." Not altogether.

Her eyebrows jogged up and down. "I like sampling the finger foods, nibbling a bit. Sucking them down. Why don't you let me?"

Dear fucking God, he was so ready for this. Too ready. He was going to embarrass himself. He'd go in his pants before he even got them down. "Raye...this won't...be good for you."

"Are you going to come in my mouth?"

"God, I hope so. Might not make it though."

She slitted her eyes and said in a rough voice, "Get up on that bench."

His eyebrows shot upward. "You going to tell me what to do?"

She puckered her lips. "You want these on you... then, yeah."

Not one to dawdle when an opportunity arose, Brian placed his hands on the workbench, pushed himself out of the chair, and swung his hips, landing his ass on bench.

She stood, used a foot to slide away the chair, then stepped between his legs.

"Um, one of us should be watching the house," he said, noting that his voice was quivering. Not exactly manly.

Her lips quirked up at one side. "I'll keep one eye

on the screen." She nodded toward his waist. "Now open up. I want dessert."

A bark of laughter surprised him. "That time it was a little much."

"The belt, sweetheart."

He went to work, desperation making him fling open the belt, and then he was tearing at the button and zipper, sliding it downward.

"Lift up a bit, and I'll ease these down," she said, gripping the waist of his jeans.

"Just to my thighs," he said, not looking at her.

Her gaze softened for a second, but then she yanked on the waistband.

He flattened his hands on the table and lifted his ass.

She slid his jeans downward, and then pushed down his boxers.

His cock sprang upward into the chilly air.

She drew a sharp breath. "I knew it was substantial..."

He moved backward on the table, between two monitors. "Why not climb on? You can skip dessert. We can both get our fill."

Her expression tightened, and she gave a sharp nod. Then she flung off her sweater and slipped off her bra.

He got a glimpse of her tits before she bent and removed her boots—dark nipples, cone-shaped. The tips were distended—perfect for sucking like a straw. When she straightened, he watched transfixed as she pushed down her jeans, shimmying out of them.

"Damn, Raye..." was all he could manage to mutter. She was a goddess. Taut, creamy skin. Muscled thighs and belly. A black thatch between her legs, trimmed in a narrow strip.

When she moved closer, he reached for her waist and brought her torso against his. Her face hovered over his, and her gaze dipped to his mouth. "I want to spend days with your mouth on me, Bri."

Feeling breathless, he whispered, "Maybe we should share a kiss first. Make sure you like how it feels."

When she laid her lips against his, he sighed into her mouth. Tears pricked his eyes, and he closed them before he betrayed the depth of his yearning. Her soft, pillowy lips moved on his, and he was lost, awash in emotions—lust, gratitude, fear, as well as hope.

He sank his fingers in her curly hair and dragged the tips against her scalp, tugging. She gave a shudder then moved closer, rubbing her chest against his shirt, and he drew back sharply and tugged off his shirt because he wanted those hard little beads rubbing against his skin. When she began to move, her entire body undulating, breasts and belly against him, he reached down to ring his cock to keep from exploding and broke off the kiss.

"You left a trail there," she said, glancing down at where he'd leaked against her belly.

"Sorry. Like I said, I don't think I'll last long."

"You don't have to," she said. She shook her head, loosening his grip, and moved away, going for the backpack again. When she held up a strip of condoms, he feared he might lose it because he felt so...he wasn't sure what, but she'd come knowing what she wanted. And for some damn reason, she wanted him.

Raydeen tore off one packet then flicked the corner open with a nail and peeled the rubber out. When she bent over his cock, he kept his grip tight around the base while she rolled it downward.

Then she squeezed her hands on his shoulders and climbed onto the bench, her knees going to either side of his hips. "Put it inside me."

He moved a hand between her legs and tentatively felt along her slit, pleased to find it wet, and then sank two fingers inside her.

She gave a groan and closed her eyes.

Encouraged, he rubbed a thumb over the top of her folds while he swirled inside her, drawing down more moisture, making sure her channel was slick and ready to take him.

Then he moved his hand to her hip and pointed his cock at her entrance. "Come down slow, Raye," he whispered. "I'll keep holding it."

"Don't. Want to slam down your dick," she said, turning her face to kiss him again. When he removed his hand, he gritted his teeth, because she was already descending, taking him deep in a single downward plunge.

"*Fuck,*" he whispered against her mouth.

"I will."

"No, *Jesus,*" he hissed.

"Don't mind if you pray, baby, but I won't have any mercy for you." Then she began to move, coming up, then lowering again, up and down. *Up and down.*

He struggled to keep aware of her. Cupped her breasts, tweaked her tips. But he was losing himself, climbing. Engulfed in slick heat, he felt his balls go hard and draw up against his groin. His thighs tightened. He wished he had feet because he would have pressed them against the floor to give some resistance so he could stroke right back, but he took everything she gave, every dip and stir, reveling in the way she moaned as she ground against him, his pubic hair scouring her clit.

When she came down harder, he couldn't hold back any longer. "Raye!" he cried out and flung back his head, stiffening as he came, filling the condom in wave after wave of release.

She didn't slow, riding his hardness, plunging down on it.

When he recovered enough to remember her pleasure, he grasped a tit and tugged on the nipple while he stroked a finger against the nugget of her clit, toggling it fast while she keened and jerked against him.

When she fell against him, he kissed her shoulder

and cradled her against his chest. "Thank you," he whispered.

She pulled back her head. "You think I was doing you some kind of favor?"

"I just meant...it's been a long time... I haven't... not since..."

"I get that, Brian. You were afraid."

He swallowed and didn't look away. "Yes. I was. I am."

She moved her hips slowly, forward and back. "I got mine, too, you know."

His mouth curved. "Glad to hear that."

Her eyes narrowed. "I don't fuck a man as part of his rehabilitation."

"Didn't think you did. But I'm grateful you chose me."

She made a grunting noise then turned her head and frowned. "There's someone taking out the trash."

He turned his head, too. "That would be Daryl. At least we know he's home."

Raydeen sighed. "I should go stick that thing to the side of his house."

"Can we stay like this a little longer?" he asked, cupping her ass and holding her down. "I think, I'm not done yet." In fact, miraculously, his cock was stirring inside her again.

She arched an eyebrow. "Wish we had a bed. I'd flip around and ride you again. Let you feel up my ass. I know you like looking at it."

"Caught me a time or two, have you?" he said, one side of his mouth quirking upward.

"Yeah," she said with a full grin. "I'm okay with it. Look all you want. Touch it, too."

"How about taste?"

Her eyes widened. "Well..."

He liked that he'd shocked her. Feeling emboldened, he said, "We'll figure this out, Raydeen. Any way I can, I'm going to have you."

"Sounds like we're going to be busy together," she said, her voice a deep rumbling purr now.

"If you like..."

"I do." She pushed on his shoulders and rose on her knees. Then she aimed a nipple at his mouth. "I've been dying to have your mouth here," she whispered.

Feeling as though he was a kid who'd been given the keys to the candy store, he bent toward her and took her deep into his mouth.

LATER, when they'd both dressed again, Raydeen rubbed her boob through her green sweater. "They ache."

"Did I bite too hard?"

"No, baby, you bit me just right. They're just not used to getting any action."

"Can't believe that. Pretty as you are."

"Oh, I've had lots of offers, but I wasn't ready." She closed up the bento box and put it to the side then retrieved the listening device from between the seats in front.

She gazed down at it and touched the switch on the back of the device. "That armed now?"

He nodded, tuning the receiver. "Say something."

"My tit aches."

He rolled his eyes when the words blasted through the van. "It works. You remember what I said?"

"Yeah. Keep to the side of the house, out of view of the windows. Stick it to the siding then come straight back. Piece of cake."

His eyebrows dipped. "Anything goes wrong..."

"Nothing's going wrong. Stop worrying. I'm goin' for a walk, is all."

With her coat buttoned and a scarf wound around her neck, she went to the passenger seat and exited the van.

She knew he was watching her as she walked away, so she added a little "extra" to her gait as she moved. Her hips felt fluid anyway, loose. Everything was loose. She'd lost her bra along the way, and her undies. Her sex was still hot and feeling a little raw from rubbing on his big dick. She held up the device. "My pussy's hot. Hope you know that's all your fault." Then she smiled because she knew he was smiling, likely feeling all cocky about the fact she'd got off on his fine-ass dick.

"I'm thinking you owe me a blow, Bri, seeing as I did most of the work. Deep tongue action. A lot of suction. Mm-mmm. Now I know what's in your pants, I'm gonna be a busy woman."

When she reached Daryl's house, she glanced up and down the road. She detected no movement. Entering the shadows, she walked as quietly as she could through the brambles. From where she stood beside the house now, she could hear a television playing. Some kind of sports program because an announcer was talking rapidly, issuing a play by play. She placed the sticky side of the device against the siding, hiding it behind a tall bush, then began to back away.

That was when she heard a low growl coming from the vicinity of Daryl's back yard. Her heart thudded against her chest wall. Fucker probably had a pit bull. She turned and began walking fast.

Brush crackled behind her, and she broke into a sprint, leaving the yard and pounding down the road. When she neared the van, the back gate opened, and she jumped inside. The door closed, but something was jumping against the side of the van, yipping.

She glanced at the monitors. The pit bull was damn short and had so much fur it looked like a dust mop.

Snorting sounded from the side. Brian was bent over the table holding his sides.

"Don't you dare laugh," she bit out.

He shook his head, but his shoulders were quivering.

"Could have been a German shepherd attack

dog. All I heard was growling. I didn't stick around to so see what it was."

"It's a..." he snickered, "a Pomeranian."

She crossed her arms over her breasts and winced because her nipples were indeed sore. "Just see if I let you bite me again."

CHAPTER 7

Brian pretended to ignore Raydeen as he continued refining the signal from the listening device. So far, all he was picking up was chatter from the TV.

Raydeen opened the bento box and began eating a bunch of grapes. "Damn, forgot how hungry sex makes me."

His mouth twitched, but again, he kept his gaze on his equipment. The next time he fucked her would be in a bed.

Inside the house, the phone rang. Uneven steps thudded on the floorboards.

"Yeah, I'm picking up a load today. Mostly pharmaceuticals. Got a doc in Helena who shorts his older customers. Have a couple friends picking up the package."

There was a pause.

"Okay, right, I'm not doing the pickup. I told you

I blew out my knee. Jim and an old friend are doing it for me... He's cool. Promise. When they get here, I'll give you a call. I'll have to do a count first so you know how much cash to bring." The sound of something tapping echoed through the van.

"Don't know why it's a problem. Sure, you haven't met him, but I told you I needed help." There was a long pause, and Daryl grunted. "Okay, you can meet him. I'm expecting them about nine.... What? That early? Look, if you don't think I can handle this..." Again, he paused. "Okay, got it." Then he slammed down the phone.

"Think he was talking about Kenan?" Raydeen asked, whispering.

"You don't have to whisper. We're a hundred yards away and inside a sound-proofed van."

"Was he talkin' about Kenan? Because it doesn't sound like his dude was happy about having a new guy to deal with."

"Maybe. I don't know." Brian raked a hand through his hair. "I think your friend might be walking into trouble. If it's even Kenan that Daryl was talking about."

She pulled her bottom lip between her teeth then released it. "What should we do?"

Brian grimaced. "I think I have to call in the big guns."

Raydeen sighed. "You mean your hunters? They really going to do this? Listen while a drug deal goes down? Should we call the cops?"

BRIAN

"Might come to that. But let me talk to Reaper first." He pulled out his phone and hit Reaper's speed dial number.

"Yo, Brian. What's up?"

"I've got a problem."

THE CLOSER IT got to nine, the more antsy Raydeen got. Brian had made his call two hours ago. Brian had placed the call on speaker because she'd been sitting too close, interrupting his conversation with Reaper with questions.

She didn't like that she'd been driving him crazy, but she was nervous. "It's 8:00. You sure your crew is on the way?"

Brian pointed toward the computer monitor. "I've been tracking their location using the GPS on their phones. Take a look," he said, turning the screen toward her. "They'll be here in under five minutes."

"Lord," she shot up from her seat, "I forgot about my bra. And my underwear. Did you see them?"

Brian gave her a sideways glance. "You flung them. They might be behind something," he said, glancing around the cramped space of the van.

She stood and began searching under the bench, in cupboards. Nothing. "Have any Glade? It smells like sex in here."

"Roll down the passenger side window and let some air in."

She dashed toward the front of the van, flipped

back the curtains, and leaned over her seat to hit the control. The window whirred down, but it was already too late. A large SUV was slowing down on the other side of the street and parking beside the curb. What looked like a dozen people spilled out of the doors.

"We have company," she whispered and dodged back behind the curtain. "Too many to fit inside here."

He hit the remote that opened the back gate of the van, which faced away from the house. Reaper stood in the opening then climbed inside, followed by Carly, Dagger, Lacey, and Hook. Not a dozen.

They crammed inside and closed the door, everyone taking a seat on the bench or a folded chair. Raydeen crossed her arms over her breasts and hoped no one noticed her nipples popping.

"Doing a little recon, Brian?" Reaper said, his eyes narrowing.

Brian cleared his throat and shot Raydeen a quick glance before turning back to Reaper, who was big enough he could have filled the space all by himself. With so many inside, she was sure all the air would be sucked out of the van. "Damn, when did it get stuffy in here?" she said, waving a hand in front of her face.

Lacey sniffed then gave Brian a wink. "Someone got busy."

"Lacey..." Brian warned.

"The ops van is not a shaggin' wagon," Dagger

said then laughed. "Good for you, bud. You, too, Raye."

"Oh my God." Raydeen placed her hands on her cheeks because they were on fire.

"We don't have time to find out who did who," Reaper growled. "What the hell kind of mess do we have here?"

"Like I said when I called," Brian said, "we think a vet Raydeen has worked with is walking into an ambush. Possibly. We set up a listening post to hear whether Kenan Reynold's buddy, whose house we staked out, talked about Kenan. What we heard concerned us. The dealer his buddy Daryl does business with wasn't too happy hearing that he had someone new on his crew. He's coming early to be here when the drugs arrive. However, we're not a hundred percent sure that Kenan Reynolds is the new guy."

"This guy worth us putting our necks out?" Reaper said, giving Raydeen a hard glance.

She swallowed. Reaper was always scary looking, but right now, if she didn't know he was a marshmallow around Carly, she might have shit herself with the hard look he gave her. "Kenan's not a bad guy. But he's got a habit. I think Daryl turned it on him and is making him earn his drugs."

"Why should I care if he's got himself in over his head?"

"Because he's not responsible for his habit. It wasn't a decision he made. Everything he got before he went rogue was prescribed. When the VA suddenly got wise about opioid abuse, they started cutting soldiers off. They left vets in a bad way without a lot of support."

"The VA would have helped him with rehab."

"I know," Raydeen said, "he didn't make the right choice, but he's not a bad person. I think he can be helped."

Reaper's mouth thinned. "We get involved, we risk our licensing. This isn't what we do." His gaze swung to Brian. "You conducted an illegal surveillance."

Brian nodded. "No excuses there. I know. But I wanted to help find this kid."

Reaper drew a deep breath and aimed another glare at Raydeen. "I'm going to make a call to Cochise's woman, Sammy. She's a deputy. Works with us sometimes. We can't say how we know..."

Brian nodded. "I'll make the call."

Raydeen closed her eyes. The last thing she'd wanted to do was add to Kenan's trouble, but after listening to the one-sided conversation Daryl had with his guy, she knew Kenan was in danger. "Do what you have to do to keep him safe."

TWENTY MINUTES LATER, Sheriff Miller and Deputy Sammy McCallister stepped inside the van. Dagger, Hook, and Carly had retreated to the SUV to let Reaper deal with the law.

"Reaper," Sheriff Miller said, giving him a solemn nod. "Sammy read me in while I driving here." His gaze went to Raydeen and Brian. "So, you were here searching for a missing vet?" He raised an eyebrow.

Raydeen cleared her throat. "I was about to knock on the front door when I overheard the conversation Daryl had with someone about drugs coming in from Bozeman. Pharmaceuticals, he said."

"And you think the soldier you're looking for is involved?"

"Not sure. But Kenan Reynolds has gone to ground," Brian said. "Hasn't been in touch with his family or the Soldiers' Sanctuary since his meds were cut. We think," he said, looking up at Raydeen, "that Daryl talked him into doing a pickup so he could get what he needed."

"And you think it's going to go down now?"

"We think Daryl's boss will arrive any time now. Kenan and another associate of Daryl's are arriving around nine."

The sheriff glanced around at the monitors in the van, which still showed the camera feeds. Brian had turned off the receiver for the listening device just before the sheriff arrived. Reaper hadn't been happy about lying to the sheriff about how they'd heard the call, but they'd agreed on the story that Raydeen happened to hear the conversation in order to keep the agency out of hot water.

Brian knew there would be a reckoning when this was over. He'd overstepped his authority, broken the law. Tonight, he might be losing his job with Montana Bounty Hunters, but he couldn't be sorry about how he'd gotten here. They were doing the right thing.

"You got more than cameras?" the sheriff asked. "Any way to listen in on what's happening inside the house?"

Brian nodded slowly.

The sheriff's eyes narrowed again. "Good. I'm going to step out. You do what you have to do while I call the judge to get the warrant."

Brian blew out a breath as the sheriff stepped out of the van.

Reaper cleared his throat. "Turn it back on."

"If this leads to an arrest..."

"I'll work it out with the sheriff. He'll contract with us for free for the use of our equipment, seeing as we're already on the scene and able. The sheriff's as eager to bust these guys as we are to see Kenan kept safe. He's not going to let a little thing like details get in the way. This is Montana law."

Brian turned on the receiver. The TV was off now. The sounds of someone walking, likely pacing the floor, came through loud and clear. It was an odd, uneven sound.

The door opened again, and the sheriff climbed back inside. "We have a warrant. A deputy is dropping by the judge's house, but we're legal...*now*." He glanced at Reaper. "I'm deputizing your hunters. I know you have earpieces and helmets with cameras. Sammy keeps me apprised of your capabilities. Let's get suited up. I've only got myself and two deputies here. I'll need your team to be our backup."

Reaper followed the sheriff outside.

Brian went to the locked boxes that served as a row of seats on the wall opposite the monitors and unlocked them. He pulled out helmets and attached cameras. By the time the hunters and the three lawmen returned, he was ready to issue them. He turned the cameras on before handing them out, one at a time, along with earpieces. "I'll need each of you to state your name as you come online, so I can synch the feeds coming through the monitors."

The sheriff stepped up again, and watched intently as the deputies and hunters called in, one at a time, and Brian typed their names so they appeared at the bottom of their feeds. Now, he could see what each of them saw.

"Wish like hell the county would spring for something like this," the sheriff muttered.

"Like I said," Reaper said, leaning into the van, "whenever you need us, we can roll out to support your guys."

"We'd need to train together."

Reaper gave a nod. "Fetch would pay for it. He'd be happy to keep our relationship thriving."

The sheriff nodded. "Well, let's get that house covered. Will we be able to hear what you're hearing?" he asked Brian.

Brian flipped a toggle switch. "Now, you will. You can talk over the feed."

When everyone departed, Brain dimmed the lights inside the van and kept watch on the monitors. He slipped a headset on to better hear the team moving in around the house, and to speak with them, should he need to.

He glanced sideways at Raydeen.

She gave him a tight smile and mouthed, "I'm okay."

They watched as the deputies and the hunters moved in the shadows, disappearing behind trees and crouching in the darkness beside the house.

The monitor trained on the street in front of Daryl's house showed a set of headlights beaming in the distance. "We've got company," Brian said softly into the mic.

"No one makes a move unless I say so," the sheriff said. "Hunker down. Have to make sure a crime is being committed."

The porch light turned on, and Daryl opened the front door, standing in the light as a black Lexus drew to a stop in front of his house.

"Brian, you get the plate?" the sheriff whispered.

"Yeah, I'll call it in to dispatch and have them run it." He zoomed in on the license plate and placed the call.

Dispatch was quick to return the identity of the owner. "That vehicle is owned by Reginald Bellows, out of Whitefish." She gave a description of Reginald as well as a long list of prior offenses, which included distribution of drugs.

Brian passed the information along to the team just as Reginald exited the back seat of the car, accompanied by his driver and a very large man.

Reginald looked up and down the street, his gaze narrowing on their van a hundred yards away, but he must not have been too worried because he strode up the driveway and onto the porch.

Daryl held out his hand. "Good to see you, Reggie, Donald, Hoss," he said the last word while looking at the largest man.

"Your guys be here soon?" came a voice that lifted the hairs on Brian's arms. It was dead even. No inflection except for a hint of menace.

Daryl glanced down at his watch. "Kenan called a minute ago. Said they stopped for gas on the edge of town. They'll be here shortly."

Raydeen drew in a sharp breath.

"So, now we know Kenan Reynold's involved," Brian said.

"Well, shit," Carly's hushed voice came over the mic.

Reginald glanced around again. "Let's wait inside."

Reginald and his minions entered the house. The door closed.

"Can I get you something to drink?" Daryl asked.

"I won't be here long enough to finish it," Reginald said.

"Sheriff, Dagger, here," Dagger broke in. "I have the back door covered."

"I'm around the side," came Sammy's voice. "I can see into the living room."

"I'm watching the bedroom window," Lacey said.

"I've got another bedroom window," Carly said.

"When the time comes," the sheriff whispered, "Landman and me'll go through the front door."

"We've got another vehicle approaching," Brian said.

A Jeep slowed as it approached the house then parked in the driveway. Two men exited. The one Brian recognized as Kenan carried a small duffel bag.

"Kenan's carrying a bag," Brian said. "He and the driver are making their way to the door."

The door opened, and once again, Daryl stood on the porch. "Well, come on in!" he said, waving the two men inside.

"Daryl, we have your delivery. We didn't have no problems. The doctor took the envelope. Said everything was fine."

"That's Kenan's voice," Raydeen said, loud enough Brian knew the rest of the team heard as well.

"I'll take that," Reginald said.

"We'll need to do a count," Daryl said, sounding upset.

"Won't be any need."

Sammy's feed bounced upward. The camera gave Brian a quick glance inside the room. His stomach tightened.

BRIAN

"Get ready," Sammy whispered. "Reginald's guys just drew their weapons. Daryl, Kenan and the other guy have their backs to me. Daryl's got a gun in the back of his pants."

"What're you doin'?" Daryl said. "You have what I promised."

"Daryl," Reginald said, this time sounding as though he was enjoying himself.

Again, gooseflesh rose on Brian's arms. The man was a sociopath.

"You know I don't like changes. We had a routine. You had one goddamn job."

"Look, everything's cool," Kenan's voice sounded. "Daryl blew out his knee. Said he needed help with a job. Everything went down just like it was supposed to. You don't have to do this."

"I like my employees to follow orders, whoever the fuck you are. *Daryl didn't.* I let one employee slide, soon everyone believes they can think for themselves. That can't ever happen."

Again, Sammy's feed shifted from the wall to the window. The man who'd been with Kenan was already on his knees, his hands behind his head. Kenan stood, his gaze going from Reginald to the two goons. Daryl's expression was stricken, his mouth slack.

"*Now,* sheriff," Sammy said. "He plans to kill all three of them."

"Landman and I are moving to the porch," the sheriff said.

Brian watched as the sheriff rose from behind the brush where he'd kept hidden and approached the front door, his arms extended, his hands cradling a gun.

Dagger raced up the back steps and stood beside the door, waiting for the signal.

Reaper and Hook moved in behind Dagger.

"I need you all on your knees," Reginald ordered.

"I blew my damn knee," Daryl shouted.

"Fucking idiot," Kenan said. "He's the one in charge. He's got the gun. Don't argue."

"Do what I say," Reginald said, his voice lowering.

"I'll have to help him down to the floor," Kenan said, his voice soft and steady.

"Kenan's moving toward Daryl," Sammy said. "He's going for the gun. I'm coming around the side of the house." Abruptly, she ducked down and moved along the side of the house, making her way toward the front.

The sheriff stood back. Deputy Landman moved in front of the door, raised a foot, and kicked it in. With his gun held out, he entered the door and moved sharply to the right.

The sheriff moved through the doorway with his gun also extended. "I'm Sheriff Miller, put down your guns!"

Reginald's gun turned toward the sheriff. The two men with him flung their bodies to the side, one disappearing behind a sofa, the larger man running down the hallway.

The sheriff's hand jerked at the same time an explosion sounded. Reginald's hand, the one holding the gun, dropped and a dark shadow blossomed on his shoulder.

Dagger's camera turned to the side, and the feed jolted. When he faced the house again, the door was hanging on its hinges, and he was moving forward.

The large man who'd raced down the hallway nearly stumbled over himself as he halted in front of Dagger and glanced toward a closed door.

"Oh no, you don't," Dagger bit out and launched himself at the man, taking him down. Fists flew, and the feed showed Reginald's man's face framed by the floor, then the ceiling, and then the floor again as the two men rolled. When the image settled, the man was on his belly and Dagger was cuffing him.

All the cameras converged, one by one, on the living room where Reginald sat, bleeding from a shoulder wound, his hands behind his back. Daryl lay on his belly, Reaper's knee in the center of his back as he was cuffed.

Sammy stood beside Kenan, who held up his hands. Brian had never seen a more lost look on a man's face. "Kenan Reynolds, you're under arrest," the deputy said.

CHAPTER 8

"Man, you screwed the pooch."

Raydeen winced as Dagger shook his head at Brian. It was well past midnight. They were back at the Montana Bounty Hunters office building, waiting for Reaper. They'd all given statements to the deputies about what they'd seen and done and had been cleared to leave, but Reaper was finishing up with the sheriff and had asked for all of them to be there when he arrived.

Brian's head was down; the droop of his shoulders betrayed the fact he must be feeling the weight of everyone's stares. She felt bad for him. She'd gotten him into this mess.

A chime sounded, and everyone glanced toward the door. Reaper and Carly strode through, their expressions grim.

Carly glanced at Raydeen. "Kenan's been booked. His father was just arriving to bail him out when we left. He said thanks for the call. Kenan is cooperating, and the sheriff said he'll put in a good word with the prosecutor."

Raydeen nodded.

Reaper walked around the counter that divided reception from the bullpen and pulled out a desk chair. He settled his large body into it and raked a hand through his long blond hair. "Dammit, Brian," he said with a huffed breath.

Brian lifted his head. "I'm not sorry."

"I get that," Reaper bit out. "That boy would be dead if you hadn't heard what you did, but still... We have rules. Laws we abide by. You've been through the training. If one of those bastards gets a really good lawyer, the case could go south, and they'll all walk. Anyone looks too close at how we heard that conversation, and we're all out of work."

Brian firmed his mouth. "I understand. It might take a day or two, but I can be packed and out of here by the weekend."

Reaper arched an eyebrow. "That right? You think I'm firing you?"

"It's what I'd do," Brian said.

Brian kept his gaze steady, his chin up, but Raydeen knew his stomach had to be in knots.

"You've built a great satellite office, here," Brian said. "I can't imagine Fetch'll be very happy about what happened tonight, either. He might reconsider placing you and Jamie in charge."

Reaper grunted. "Well, it's a good thing I had

Jamie sit this one out. Told her she was too close to you. That I didn't need her here fighting for you."

Brian's eyes grew glossy, but he blinked them dry. "I imagine she'd try. But you needn't worry about what she'll say to you. I'll make it easy. I quit."

The other hunters stirred in their seats, but they stayed silent, their gazes turning to Reaper.

"Well, not so fast, buddy," Reaper said, sitting forward in his chair. "It's true; Fetch isn't happy. I spoke to him when I finished with the sheriff. Thing is, he didn't like the fact you stepped outside the law, but he did like your initiative. And your instincts. He also said, not that I needed to hear it, that a lot of our success rests on your shoulders. You're the heart of this office, Brian. Have been since the day we brought you in. I don't want to lose you. But I have to know you won't go off on your own again." He raised his hands. "I'm not saying you can't take out the van. I'm also not saying you can't perform surveillance on your own. You've proven you can, but any job you do as a *hunter*, has to be on the books."

Brian frowned. "As a hunter?"

Reaper shrugged. "It's what you are. When you make calls, you're doing our work. When you surveil or provide support, you're part of our team. You're a hunter, Brian, same as us."

Brian's shoulders rose, and he drew a deep breath. "But tonight..."

"Yeah, there has to be a consequence. Fetch figured you should take a few days off, and that your pay ought to be docked what it'll cost to pay the team for their time."

Brian nodded. "Sounds more than fair," he said, his voice hoarsening.

"Might want to think about getting out of the office for a while," Reaper said, his gaze going to Raydeen.

The way he looked at her, with a gleam in his eye, told her everything she needed to know. Reaper wasn't angry. And he was doing Brian a favor here. "He can stay at my place. Seein' as how I'm the reason he's in trouble."

Brian's head swung toward her. His gaze was steely, but she couldn't read his expression. She couldn't be sure he was happy with her offer.

"Well, seems it's all settled," Reaper said. "Carly and Jamie will watch the office while you're out. Not that we're being sexist or anything, but we know those two can work the computers without going to blue screens." He pushed up from his chair then strode toward Brian, holding out his hand.

Brian shook it and gave him a solemn look. "I won't fuck up again."

"Oh, I'm sure you will. We all do." He gave Brian a wink then turned on his heel, skirting the counter and heading toward the door. Carly pushed up, flashed Brian a smile, and followed him out.

Lacey gathered her latest Michael Kors' tote and bent to kiss Brian's cheek. "Enjoy the time off," she whispered loudly. Then she straightened and waggled her eyebrows at Raydeen, before leaving with Dagger.

Hook gave them a casual salute and left as well.

When it was just the two of them, Raydeen drew in a deep breath. "I'm so sorry."

"Stop." Brian gave her a sideways glance.

Fuck, was he angry with her? "I shouldn't have asked you for a favor."

"Raye. Stop," he repeated.

"But—"

He reached out, grabbed her arm, then pulled her sideways over the handrail of his wheelchair and straight onto his lap.

She landed hard, her hair falling forward. When she reached up to push it back, she found his face in the way. His mouth hovered over hers. "I'm not sorry," he whispered. "I'm glad I could help you. I'd do anything for you."

Raydeen's heart raced. "Good to hear," she said faintly. She couldn't think of anything witty to say because she was staring at his lips and remembering how they'd felt latched around her nipple as he'd sucked her "like a straw"—his description. *Lucky fucking straw.*

His eyes narrowed.

"I say that out loud?"

"Uh huh."

A hand crept under the hem of her green sweater, smoothed over her ribs, then cupped her breast. She hissed a breath when his fingers pinched the tip.

"That hurt?" he asked, his voice deepening.

"Hurts just right." She tapped his bottom lip. "But I know what could make it feel so much better."

"We have to be out of here come morning," he said, bending and nuzzling her cheek.

She shivered. "Won't take me long, baby. I've been hot ever since I watched you workin' that console in the van, lookin' so fuckin' intense."

"I've been hot for you since the day we met. Doesn't matter what you do, what you wear, I've imagined taking you every way humanly possible and few that aren't quite human. Now, every time I see you in green, I'm gonna think about these little gems," he said, tweaking her nipple, "popping against your sweater while you tried to take the rap for me with Reaper."

She wrinkled her nose. "Damn, I forgot I wasn't wearin' a bra."

"I think everyone knew you weren't. And I have a secret."

She liked the way his mouth curved as he gave her a boyish smile. "What's that?"

"I'm sitting on your bra and panties."

She slapped his shoulder. "You had them all the time I was lookin' for them?"

"Yeah, I had them under my ass because I liked looking at your breasts."

"Huh." She pouted her lips but couldn't hold

back a giggle. "Have a thing for women's underwear?"

"I do for yours."

"I'm okay with that. You can sit on any old thing you want so long as I get to sit on your fine-ass dick."

"Baby, I love the way you talk."

"I love the way you feel, crowding up inside me," she growled. When he gave her nipple another twist, she arched her back. "Your mouth...please..."

His hand swept up her sweater, and he bent to take her aching tip between his lips. When he sucked, she felt moisture flood her channel. "I'm gonna need some clean clothes, because I just soaked my jeans."

His muffled laughter shook against her body, and she wound her arms around his shoulders. "Take me to your bed, Bri."

SHE STRIPPED beside the mattress while he braked his chair and gracefully lifted himself from his seat to the bed. By the time she stood nude, he'd only managed to remove his shirt. His broad chest, with its cloak of sparse dark hair, beckoned. She couldn't wait to rest her cheek against it, to tease his nipples like he had hers.

But she needed to talk him out of jeans. She knew he was self-conscious about removing them. Likely, he didn't want her to see his scarred stumps, but it was up to her to prove to him that she didn't care. That she saw him as a sexy man from the top his head to the end of his damaged legs.

She crawled onto the end of the mattress and walked on her hands and knees toward him, knowing he was watching her boobs sway beneath her, the tips fully engorged. When she reached his legs, she spread her knees to crawl over his body until she could sit on his clothed hips. She shook back her curls and reached for his hands, placing them on her breasts. "That's better," she said, leaning into his embrace. "I love it when you touch them. They get hard. The tips throb. And then all I can think about is having your mouth on them."

He pulled on her breasts and brought her down. She rose a little on her knees and aimed a nipple at his lips.

He lifted his head and rooted at it, latching hard around the areola. Then he used his teeth to gently torture her, alternately chewing on the tip and tapping it with his tongue. He was driving her crazy. Fluid filled her slit. "I'm wet for you, Brian."

A hand glided down her belly and fingers slid between her folds. A groan vibrated against her breast as he fingered her entrance then slipped inside her.

She squeezed around him, holding him inside, inviting him deeper. When he gasped and kissed his way across her chest, she figured maybe he was far enough along she could get him past his reticence. His jeans had to go. *Now*.

She drew back and moved to the side. Glancing down at his jeans, she said, "Lose them."

His cock jerked inside pants, but he held his breath.

"I've seen stumps," she said, "you know I have. I'm not gonna think less of you. I don't want anything between us."

He drew in a breath that lifted his broad chest then reached for his belt and opened it. She reached for the button at the top of his waistband, flicked it open, then slowly slid the zipper down, liking the scratchy sound of it, because it was loud inside the very quiet room.

They both held their breaths.

Brian gave a groan and dug his covered stumps into the mattress to lift his hips. He pushed his jeans to midway down his thighs, exposing himself.

"Nice," she said, giving his erect cock a stroke. "Now, the rest of the way."

He lowered his hips and lifted his legs, tugging off the garment then tossing it to the floor. Then he lay still, his hands curling into the bedding while she looked at him, taking in his chest, his belly, his glorious cock and hips, his strong thighs, his knees... the savaged stumps.

The incisions were white. Well healed. The length of each limb beneath the knee almost even.

She lifted her chin toward his legs. "Open them."

"Bossy," he said, his voice sounding strained, but he spread his legs.

She moved between them and knelt. Then because she wanted him thinking about the prize, if he was a good boy, she flung back her head and massaged her breasts. "I like the way you play with these. You're gentle...then you're not. Like you know I won't break. I like it when they're tugged," she said, pulling on a tip and letting it go, enjoying the bounce. "I fucking love your teeth on me," she said, twisting a tip. "When they're hard, the way you nibble them...I feel it all the way to here..." She cupped her pussy and trailed a fingertip along her slit. She swirled her fingers in the moisture she coaxed from inside her body then trailed a wet finger along the inside of his thigh, downward, past his knee.

"Raye..." he warned, but while his expression tightened, his eyes let her see inside his soul. He needed acceptance. Hers. Needed her to be alright with the damage to his body, so she lifted one leg, and fit the appendage between her legs and rubbed against it, letting him feel how wet she was. "Straighten it," she said, and then pushed it right against her pussy, moving on it like she was fucking it. "Brian, look at me," she said, because his gaze had gone to the ceiling. "Watch," she said as she rubbed and rubbed, the thickness between her legs getting her hotter and hotter.

"Stop it, Raye."

"Why, baby? Can't you tell I want to fuck you, every part of you. I want to lick you up and down. Taste you."

He bared his teeth and cupped his balls. "I have a better place for you to start."

Lowering his leg, she widened her knees and slid her pussy up his leg, pausing at his knee to undulate, then moving upward to his thick thigh. The muscles twitched against her, and she bent her head to kiss his belly, rimmed his bellybutton with her tongue, then moved between his legs again, because she was growing impatient to feel his cock in her mouth. His big cock jerked as she ran her tongue up one side then down the other. She gripped it hard and bent to lick his balls, wetting the hair and skin, then sucking one orb into her mouth. She mouthed it, rolling it on her tongue then opened her mouth and captured the other ball.

Brian cussed under his breath and raised his legs, balancing them on his stumps as he gave shallow pumps of his hips. She knew what he wanted—what his motions invited. She pushed up on her arms and took the tip of his cock inside her mouth and slid her tongue over the cap, lapping around and around. When she pointed her tongue and nudged the eyelet slit, he hissed and gripped her hair.

She teased him for a long time, sucking, "chewing", licking only the cap and the delicate underside, until he pulled harder on her hair. The dull pain caused her to groan. She loved it. Wanted more of it. When he pulled again, forcing her down, she relented, sinking down on him, letting his shaft slide across her tongue to the back of her throat. When she gagged, he held still, waiting.

Swallowing, she opened her throat and sank some more, letting him deeper into her throat while she gripped his balls and rolled them in her palm, massaging, tugging, while she bobbed up and down.

When she glanced up at him, she found that he'd lifted his head and was watching her, his gaze fierce. Gone was the little boy lost. A feral man clutched her hair, and he wanted everything from her now. She held his gaze as she sank then sucked hard when she came up. After she did that a few more times, she pulled back, coming off him.

Breathing hard and braced on her arms over his cock, she met his stare. "Will you fuck me, Brian? Give it to me good?"

He pulled her hair, forcing her up his body then swept his free arm around her back and brought her against him. His kiss was bruising and left her breathless. Then he rolled with her, and his body was on top of hers. She spread her legs, bent her knees, and placed her hands on his ass.

When he raised himself above her, resting on his hands and knees, they both glanced down their bodies.

"Funny," she whispered, "this view's the same whether a man has ankles or not." She lifted her gaze to his, challenging him.

His chest billowed with his deep breaths. He bent and kissed her again, this time simply sucking at her lips, drawing on them to seal their kiss. When he broke off, he spoke into her ear, "Raydeen, I'm not fucking cloaked."

She laughed, because she heard disgust in his voice. "I'm clean, Brian. Not on the pill, but then, I don't care about consequences. I'm ready for them. Are you?"

When he pulled back to look into her face, the look in his eyes nearly broke her heart.

"Baby, did you think I was only in this for the sex?" she whispered.

He blinked hard. "You want kids? With me?"

She placed her palm alongside his cheek. "I see you, Brian. I see how lonely you are. We both are. Together, we can have everything our hearts yearn for."

His jaw hardened. "What I yearn for, right this second," he said, his voice as rough as sandpaper, "is to be buried inside you."

She bounced her hips against him. "Then come right on in, baby."

CHAPTER 9

Brian schooled his face into a hard mask. It was that or lose it completely. She was right. Looking down at their bodies, they could be any man or woman. He couldn't see his missing legs. His cock jutted toward her belly, her abdomen quivered as she raised her knees and tilted her wet pussy, ready to receive him.

What she'd said about consequences had struck his heart, too.

He'd never considered having children. Hell, he'd never considered having a woman in his life, not after he'd been wounded. He'd thought he'd adjusted to his new normal, learning to adapt to a wheelchair, doing a job that mattered, but he'd only been living half a life. He realized that now, gazing down at her. At them.

She nudged his cock with her mound, and he

moved his hips, lowering them, and then pushing forward between her folds, sliding into her entrance. With a jerk of his hips, he thrust inside her, filling her channel, stroking until he was sunk as deep as he could go. He sucked in a breath.

Her fingernails dug into his ass. "Don't stop now," she said, giving a breathless laugh.

"Couldn't if I tried," he muttered. "You feel... amazing, like wet silk, baby. Hot, slick." He pulled out and drove forward again. "Fuck, you feel..." But he couldn't hold onto the thought, because she squeezed around him, and he had to move faster and faster.

He felt as though he was running a race, his lungs filling with and expelling air, his ass and thighs getting tighter and tighter. Soon, he was hammering against her...fast, hard.

She wiggled under him, trying to raise her legs. He paused and hooked her knees with his arms, then pounded her again, loving the way it felt, his groin crashing against her vulva as his cock pistoned inside her.

He'd never ridden a woman bareback. Never dared. The difference was stunning. Or maybe it was just knowing this could lead to something, be something bigger than he was, than they were. It made the moment poignant, momentous. He wanted this woman. Forever. He'd do what he could to make sure she had plenty of reasons to stick around. Maybe he'd need some advice to figure out what those reasons might be.

When her head began to thrash on the pillow and her moans lengthened, he knew she was close. He let go of her legs and came down on his elbows, framed her face with his hands, and kissed her. His strokes became shorter, harsher, as he tunneled in her wet heat.

"Brian!" she cried, breaking the kiss. Her neck arched. He felt the ripples, up and down her channel, the soft convulsions her pussy made as she came. He gave her two more strokes then held still, his jaws locking closed as his come streamed in rhythmic pulses, filling her womb.

When he collapsed atop her body, they lay wrapped in each other's arms while their breaths deepened and grew quieter.

Raydeen raked his scalp with her nails. "That was some fucking, mister."

Chuckling, he lifted his head. "I'm glad you approve."

Her gaze fell away. "What I said before..."

He turned his head and kissed the inside of her wrist. "I'm okay with consequences."

When her gaze returned to his, she simply stared back. "Good. Because...well, I'm ready, Brian...for whatever comes next. But maybe this is too soon for you...?"

He sighed and rested on his elbows. His cock was

deflating and beginning to retreat. His brain was taking over. "I think...I might be ready to let you get me fitted with legs. If I'm going to be a hunter...and someday, a father...I don't want to accept being less than I can be."

She tsked and tugged his ear. "Silly man. You were never less. If I'd thought for a second you wanted to be in that chair for the rest of your life, I wouldn't have pushed. I swear. There's so much you can do, so much you've already accomplished. Don't do this for me or any kids we might make along the way. Do it for you. Only for you."

Brian leveled a steady gaze on her. "I've been hiding in my chair. Making myself indispensable, yes, but accepting less of what I want because I didn't think I deserved anything more. I certainly never thought I'd deserve someone like you."

She blinked. "Why? I'm not that special."

"Beg to differ, ma'am. You've made a big difference in many soldiers' lives. You're making a difference in mine." He shrugged. "It's cliché to say it, but I feel guilty. I lost my legs, but a friend of mine lost his life in the same explosion. His name was Benny. He was the funniest guy I ever met. A good friend. Always had my back. But I didn't have his when that IED hit."

"Well, I don't know what happened, baby, but I know you. There's no way you're any way responsible for his death."

"I *know* that. I do. But that's not how I *feel*."

She gave him a sad smile. "I like that we're having

this conversation while your dick is still inside me. Feels like we have to tell the truth, doesn't it?"

He swept an arm beneath her to cuddle her closer. "The FBI should conduct their lie detector tests like this."

"They'd certainly get some interesting results," she drawled. Then she sighed. "You know I was married, right?"

He nodded. "Some of the guys at the sanctuary told me. Said your husband was killed."

She drew a deep breath. "Mike was wounded by artillery. He lost a leg and a hand. I was with him at Walter Reed when he took his own life. I have my own guilt. I didn't fight hard enough or give him reason enough to live."

Brian kissed her to shut her up. He didn't like seeing the glimmer of tears in her eyes. When he lifted his head, he gave her a scowl. "You were not responsible for his choice. Whether he wasn't brave enough to face his limitations or simply had experienced enough pain, it was his choice."

She sniffed. "I know that. Still, I became a physical therapist, working with vets, because I felt like I'd failed."

"Well, aren't we a pair?" He gave her a tender smile. "We both have our scars."

A tear ran across her temple into her hair. He used his thumb to dry it.

Again, she sniffed. "Are you sure you want prosthetics?"

He thought for a moment and let the idea play around his head. Before, he'd said it without really thinking, but now, he was pretty sure he'd spoken straight from his heart. "Yeah, I think I'm ready. But only if you're my therapist."

She frowned. "Most dudes I work with end up cussin' me out. They apologize after, but I push hard."

"I can't see me cussing you out, babe, and I don't want you going easy on me. I need to do this. Just remind me why every once in a while," he said, giving her a sexy nudge below.

"I think I can do that," she said, a smile stretching slowly across her face. "When you're bone tired and aching, I'll do all the work. Maybe I'll trade blow jobs for the number of steps you take."

"You might have to conduct my therapy after hours."

She giggled and slid her fingertips down his spine. "I'm pretty sure there are cameras all over the place."

"Then we'll have to make do with a dressing room."

"I like the places your imagination goes." She cupped his buttocks with her hands and dug her fingernails deep into the muscles.

His cock stirred inside her. "Raye, I've daydreamed about fucking you in places all over this town."

"I'm happy doing it again, right here, right now."

"Hate to break it to you, but I'm only half-hard, sweetheart."

"It's my job to get your dick interested." She spanked one of his cheeks. "Roll onto your back."

"Yes, ma'am." He eased out of her and moved beside her on the mattress. He placed an arm beneath his head and cupped his balls with his other hand.

Raydeen leaned over him and smoothed her cheek on his chest. "Soft hair. I like it," she said, then licked a nipple.

His nipples were more sensitive than he'd ever realized as she plied them with her tongue and lips, sucking them until the centers formed hard points. While she played there, her hand trailed down to his dick, and she wrapped her fingers around him, gently tugging and stroking while his shaft thickened.

When he was fully hard, she moved toward his hips, but instead of turning to face him, she straddled him backwards, holding his cock up while she slowly swirled her hips and screwed downward, taking him inside her. When she was fully settled, she glanced over her shoulder. "I know you like my ass," she said. "I'm okay with you playin' there."

Brian reached for a second pillow and stuck two beneath his head and shoulders, the better to watch as he gripped the fleshy globes, massaging them as she began to rise and fall. She was a well-built woman, with firm muscle beneath the soft flesh. The shape of her back, which narrowed at her waist and flared generously at her hips, was damn close to perfection for him.

He enjoyed the sight of his cock, glistening with her moisture, as it appeared then disappeared with every rise and fall of her body. He held her cheeks apart to get a better view and realized that when he did, her breaths grew jagged. She hadn't been exaggerating, she really liked to be touched there.

He cupped a palm and clapped it against one cheek, not hard, but it made a satisfying thud.

Her body shivered, and her movements grew less fluid. But she didn't mouth a complaint. So, he did it again, this time flattening his hand to deliver a stinging slap.

She cried out and swayed. Moisture flooded her channel.

He slapped the other side, then alternated the claps, watching as her tawny skin reddened. When her breaths became even more broken, he slid a wet finger between her cheeks and pressed it against her tight ring, just fluttering it there, waiting for her reaction, for her to tell him to stop, but when she bent and cupped his knees, giving him better access, he pushed inside her.

"*Oh fuck, fuck, fuck,*" she chanted going still.

"Raye, do you need me to take over?" he said, his voice rough.

"Can't move. Feels so fuckin' good." Her voice was almost a whine, which made him smile.

"I want you on your hands and knees, baby."

BRIAN

She straightened and let his cock slide from inside her, then fell forward to rest on her elbows.

Brian slid from under her and went to his knees behind her. He parted her buttocks and dropped spit on her anus. Then he fed his cock into her pussy while he slipped two fingers into her ass. Gripping one hip, he began to move, thrusting his fingers and his cock in unison, fucking into both entrances. "Someday soon, I'm gonna have that ass, Raye. And you're gonna let me."

"Bet you'll make me beg," she said, sinking her chest to the bed. "God, I wish you had four hands. I need them on my tits, too."

He chuckled, but the sound was strained, because his cock was gripped by her convulsing inner muscles. While swirling his fingers in her ass, he pumped his hips, jerking them at the end of each stroke to give her a jolt. Her breaths gusted, and the sounds she made, groans interspersed with whimpers, made him feel more of a man than he ever had. He was doing this, giving her what she needed, controlling her rising passion. Legs or no legs, he could fuck her just like she wanted. Hard and fast. "How about you play with your tits? Slap them."

"Wanna see me do it, lover?"

He paused his strokes and glanced sideways at the mirror on his dresser. He grunted. This wouldn't be his smoothest move, but... "Let's turn toward the mirror." When she moved too quickly, she nearly pulled free of his cock, so he clamped his hand on her hip and held her against his groin while they shuffled to face the mirror.

"You see us?" she said, pushing up on her arms.

He gave her several hard strokes and watched the way her tits jiggled.

"Oh, yeah," she said biting her lower lip. "We need mirrors everywhere, babe. I wanna see your ass flex when you fuck me."

"Not turning again," he muttered.

She gave a gusting laugh. "You wanted to see me slap something, didn't you? Watch me." Supported on one arm, she slapped her breast then held it up, letting him see the erect tip. My tits are big enough, I have a special talent," she said, waggling her eyebrows. "Let me come up, and I'll show you."

Brian was desperate to see, so he removed his fingers from her ass and gripped her waist on both sides to bring her up. Now she sat on his dick, but he could see the entire front of her body. She molded a breast with both hands and pulled it upward while at the same time craning her neck and reaching out with her tongue.

When she licked her own nipple, he gave a hoarse grunt. "Baby, suck it."

She rolled her eyes. "My lips can't reach that far."

"Damn. Do it again."

She toggled the hard tip, all the while glancing at him in the mirror. Her mouth curved, and she raised her head. "Did you like it?"

Brian laughed. "When you masturbate, is that something you do to please yourself?"

She pressed her lips together. "Guess you'll have to catch me at it to know."

"You're a tease, Raydeen Pickering."

She raised an inch and squeezed down on his cock. "You're not as deep like this, but this position does have its perks." She cupped her breasts and held them up, jiggling them on her palms.

He kissed the side of her neck while he watched her in the mirror. "We'll need to make a stop at an adult toy store."

"Something you want to buy?" she asked, rotating her hips.

"Nipple clamps, for starters."

She pursed her lips. "Sounds painful." Then she grinned. "I might like that." She bounced on his cock. "Just thinking about it makes me hot."

He gripped her waist and moved her up and down his shaft, watching as she squeezed the tips of her breasts and stretched them while he moved her energetically up and down, causing her breasts to bounce while she held the tips immobile.

"Oh, yeah, keep doing that," she said, giving a shiver. "The look in your eyes, baby."

"Can't see me," he bit out. He was watching her eyes, narrowed to slits; her mouth pursed as she panted.

When she came, he gave a shout and slammed her downward, holding her as tightly to his groin as he could while he exploded. When they both went still, he looped his arms around her belly and hugged her against him. "We better pack."

"Don't need but one set of clothes," she said, opening her eyes and grinning. "We're spending the rest of the week in bed."

"Your job?" he said, arching an eyebrow.

She fake-coughed. "I have a helluva bad cold."

CHAPTER 10

On Monday morning, Brian sat at the table in the agency's kitchen. Everyone was there, including Felicity, Hook's girlfriend, who ran the website; Cochise's woman, Deputy Sammy McCallister, since she worked part-time for the agency; and Tamara Adams, who was Quincy's fiancée, and helped out in the office. The production crew was due to arrive any minute now, so Reaper had texted the entire crew and all the support personnel to be there.

Brian had been the first in the kitchen and had started the coffee. Raydeen hit the bakery and bought donut bribes to make sure everyone had a sweetened disposition for the morning meeting, then she left to head back home to get ready for work. It was her first day back following her sick leave, and karma was a bitch, because she'd started sneezing the night before.

"Let's get this rodeo started." Reaper glanced at

Jamie. He didn't like running meetings, and always let her take the lead.

She set her cheese Danish on her plate and folded her hands. "As you all know from our previous experience with the film crew, things are about to get crazy. We've gotten used to them being around while we work, but we need to make sure they don't take advantage of that fact. They might also be feeling like they know how things work, but we don't want anyone getting hurt. Don't be shy about calling them out when they get in the way of things.

"If you recall from our last meeting with them in the fall, this season they want our viewers to get to know us better."

There were groans around the room. Brian shook his head. No one would dread the intrusion of the film crew more than him. "Rosalie seems eager to get into our bedrooms," he muttered.

"Well, yours is likely the be the busiest right about now, so maybe she should spend the season with you," Reaper said, giving Brian a smirk.

"Um, no."

"So, you and Raydeen...finally?" Tamara said, raising both eyebrows.

Brian rolled his eyes, unwilling to let any of the women start in on him.

Hook chuckled. "This means I won't have to freeze my ass off at the track quite so often."

"'Bout damn time," Quincy said smiling. "The

place used to stink of pheromones whenever you two were in the same room."

"Ha!" Lacey laughed. "Should have been in the van last Friday ni—"

Brian cleared his throat and gave Lacey a frown.

She pretended to zip her mouth shut, but her eyes were laughing.

Brian shifted in his seat. "Although they will definitely not be welcome in my bedroom, they might want to spend a little extra time with me."

Reaper glanced his way. "Why's that?"

"Because..." Brian grimaced because he knew the team was about to get loud, "I asked Raydeen to look into seeing how soon I can get some new legs."

Silence followed, surprising him.

Jamie leaned forward and patted his hand. "Good for you. However much time you need off, it's all sick leave."

"Yeah, Brian," Lacey said, coming around the table. "Hell, if they want us to donate our time off, I'll give you every hour of mine. Congratulations." And she kissed his cheek.

Smiles appeared. Hook gave him a thumbs up with his left thumb. "You'll have the best therapist, too, although you'll be cussing her—"

Brian shook his head. "No, I won't. I know it won't be easy, but I won't abuse her."

"Just sayin'," Hook said, shrugging, "we all get testy when we're being pushed hard, and it gets kind of emotional."

"I'll be fine."

"I'll make sure Raydeen has someone to vent to," Jamie drawled. When he gave her a glare, she grinned.

"Back to the subject," Reaper growled.

"Of Brian's rehab?" Lacey asked.

"Oh, do we have someone with a drug problem?" Rosalie said from the doorway.

Brian groaned. Once the *Bounty Hunters of the Northwest* director seized on a topical theme, she was like a pit bull with a chew toy.

"You're just in time," Jamie said, rising to greet Rosalie, but only after turning to make a face at the group, telling them silently to behave themselves. "No, no one's going through that kind of rehab. We were just discussing the fact that Brian is going to be fitted for prosthetics and learning how to use them."

Rosalie's large doe eyes widened as they settled on Brian. "How fantastic! A recovering vet! I see Emmy nominations! Or at the very least, a visit with Ellen!"

The team laughed at her excitement. Reaper reached out and patted Brian's shoulder. "This is perfect payback, man."

Brian shook his head. *Well, hell...*

THREE DAYS LATER, Andrew Willoughby, the prosthetist, was having a hard time pretending a cameraman wasn't filming his every move. A hard task, seeing as he was seated on a rolling stool in front of Brian as he measured his stumps.

"Just do what you normally do," Edgar Rivera, the camera man, said, after Andrew dropped his tape measure for the third time. "Forget I'm here."

Andrew gave Brian a baleful look. "How do you do it?" he whispered to Brian.

Brian shrugged. "You get used to it." And he had. After all, as soon as Rosalie had learned what Brian was planning to do, she'd attached herself to him like a leech. For the past few days, Rosalie and Edgar had broken away from the rest of the production crew to follow him around in his apartment from the time he hit his alarm at the start of the day, brushed his teeth, fixed the thermostat, and then rolled into the agency's kitchen. They'd sat beside him as he'd made cold calls, answered inquiries, met with bail bondsmen—all his daily shit—then they'd accompanied him and Raydeen to dinner, documenting every inconvenient little detail of his life.

They'd wanted to get the "before" routine on film then follow him through the process of being fitted, and then learning to walk on his new legs. Thank goodness, they thought they'd have enough "before" by the time this day ended, so they could concentrate on some other couple in the agency and leave him and Raydeen the hell alone.

Then maybe they could have some real *alone time*, aka sex.

After going years without any, the last few days

of abstinence had frayed every last one of his nerves. Not that he thought Edgar or Rosalie would have minded if they'd had to fade to black once he and Raydeen were in bed. Rosalie had told him point blank that people liked to know how "you folks" do everything.

Not that Brian was offended by being called "you folks"—Rosalie was brisk and blunt, but didn't have a mean bone in her body. Still, he was pretty sure with the way they'd already filmed his transfers from bed to chair to toilet, kindly leaving him alone before he pushed down his boxers, that their audience would be able to figure out that there would be some adjustments for sex.

Not many, as it turned out, seeing as Raydeen was perfectly comfortable straddling him when they did it on the bathroom counter. He'd even hung from a chin-up bar to take her against the doorframe. He didn't want her to ever regret not being boned standing up.

"Andrew, tell Edgar and Rosalie why these measurements are so important," Raydeen said from her position near the doorway. She made it a point to be with Brian through every step of the process. Not something she usually did, because she trusted the other staff, but he was her boyfriend, dammit. Brian kind of liked how possessive she was. Her hovering tended to get things done quicker, too.

Andrew fitted the measuring tape around the end of the stump to measure the circumference. "The manufacturer needs exact numbers. They fashion a urethane and gel liner to fit over the residual limb. The fit has to be close to perfect because there can't be any air bubbles between his skin and the liner or they'll cause blisters and sores. They'll construct a prosthetic that will be close to a perfect fit, but not exact because a residual limb—"

"Andrew, you can say *stump*," Brian whispered overloud.

Andrew frowned at him. He'd likely been through too much sensitivity training to ever be natural with his patients. "The prosthetic is left a little larger because the size of the *residual limb* fluctuates throughout the day, so the artificial limb has to accommodate socks over the liner to help with those fluctuations."

Andrew's discomfort was forgotten while he spoke because he took measurements farther up his stump and from the knee around the bottom of the stump and up to the back of the knee without dropping the tape again. Then he repeated the process on Brian's other leg.

"How long will it take for the prosthetics to be shipped back for Brian to try them out?" Rosalie asked.

"About three weeks."

She frowned. "Any way they can come faster?"

Andrew glanced upward. "No, that's how long it takes."

Rosalie huffed, but didn't try to argue with the man.

When he'd finished with all the measurements and they'd completed all the forms, Brian could tell Rosalie was bored. "You know, you don't have to stick around. I'm just going to be doing some floor exercises with Raydeen for about an hour before I head back to the office."

"Can you do those back at your place later?" Rosalie asked, giving them a sly look.

Raydeen held up a hand next to her mouth and pretended to whisper to Brian. "She wants to see us make out after I make you sweat."

"I got that," Brian said. He shrugged. "Babe, it's completely up to you."

Raydeen smiled. "I'll bring a yoga mat."

RAYDEEN COUNTED as Brian completed his sixtieth sit up. She'd hunkered down and placed his legs over her shoulders while she gripped them to hold them against her body while he pumped up and down. Brian was pretty sure this wasn't the way she conducted these exercises with her other patients, but any excuse to get her hands on him was one she'd take. She'd confessed that she too had been feeling a little snippy due to their lack of intimacy of late.

When he rested on the mat, she moved his legs off then lay beside him. She too was dressed in bike shorts and a tank for the workout. "Let's do some lateral crunches, now."

Brian glanced sideways and gave her a mean look.

She returned a perky smile. "Isn't this fun?"

"So, why the workouts, Raydeen?" Rosalie asked. She sat on the edge of the armchair in Brian's bedroom.

Brian thought she was kind of cute in a nerdy way. Rosalie Saucedo was wiry and slim, medium height. Her dark brown hair was wavy and usually pulled back in a tight pony tail. She rarely wore makeup and always dressed in what he'd call her "director's uniform"—khaki pants, a three-quarters sleeved Henley, a khaki vest with lots of pockets, and hiking boots. When she followed the team into the woods on a hunt, she added a floppy, military-style hat.

He guessed she was in her late thirties, but it was hard to gauge a number because she had very few lines on her pretty oval face.

"Brian needs to strengthen his core, buttocks, and thighs to help him maintain his balance once he's up on his prosthetics."

"Looks like he's already in pretty good shape," Rosalie said, eyeing Brian's muscled chest and abdomen.

The tank he wore looked glued to his body because he'd sweated so much. Every hill and hollow were nicely defined. "He's in great shape, but it doesn't hurt to keep honing those muscles. It'll make his time in rehab shorter."

"I read somewhere that the life expectancy of an amputee is ten to fifteen years less than a normal person's."

By the way her back stiffened, Brian was pretty sure that comment had Raydeen's hackles rising.

"First," she said, "an amputee *is* a normal person. Second, that ten to fifteen-year loss occurs when amputees don't up their cardio. It's a vascular issue that aerobic exercise helps. Brian plays basketball and rolls around the track. Plus, based on his abs," she said, patting his belly, "he's been exercising on his own—a lot."

"What will his rehab experience look like? How long is the process of getting him used to his new legs going to take?"

Raydeen smiled at Brian. They'd already discussed it. He knew it was going to be a long and arduous journey, lasting up to a year. "It'll be like taking baby steps. The first day, he'll only wear his new prostheses for a total of two hours. Only half an hour of that will be with him standing on them. When he does stand on them, we'll have to check his residual limbs every fifteen minutes for swelling and to see how his skin is doing."

She reached for his hand and held it. "Each day we'll add more time, until we're adding an hour more of use every day. And there may be setbacks. If he has issues with sores and seepage, we'll have to work with the prosthetist to make adjustments to the thickness of the socks, to the artificial limb, or get a new liner. It takes time, but the end result will be added mobility. Depending on the style of limb he uses, he will be able to walk, run, climb... It's entirely up to him."

Brian gave her a smile, telling her silently that he held not a shadow of doubt that he'd get there. "What's next?"

She went to her knees, bracketed his face with her hands, and kissed him.

As the kiss deepened, Rosalie cleared her throat. "Will he be able to drive using his artificial legs?"

Raydeen turned her head, snuggling her cheek against Brian's as she answered, "No. Since he can't feel the pedals, and he lost both legs, he'll still need to use hand controls when he's driving."

Brian liked that she seemed to need to touch him quite a lot. "But I'll be able to move more easily around the van, out of the van, even set up my own surveillance gadgets without needing someone else to trek through the weeds." He turned his face to kiss her palm. "I might not be able to chase down a target on foot, but I can definitely do more of the physical work."

Rosalie smiled. "I've already seen you at work in your van, tracking your team on those monitors while you're typing a mile a minute on a keyboard, or flying those nifty drones. I'd say they're pretty lucky to have someone with your skills."

Brian tipped his chin. "I'd say they're pretty lucky, too."

"We should shower," Raydeen said. "I'll go first. While you're in, I'll start dinner." She turned to Edgar and Rosalie. "I'm making chicken enchiladas with green chili sauce. Hope you two like jalapenos."

Rosalie clapped. "The hotter the better, but you don't have to cook for us."

"Since this is your last night with us," Raydeen said, pointedly, "I thought we'd celebrate."

Rosalie tilted her head and gave the couple a sly smile. "That's so thoughtful. Don't suppose we could get some kind of intimate fade to the bedroom shots before we leave...?"

Brian chuckled. "By the end of dinner, I don't think either of us will even notice you're here..."

CHAPTER 11

Six weeks later, Brian sat in the ops van with Edgar sitting on a low stool beside him, his camera leaning on his shoulder. It was a Saturday, and Raydeen had ridden shotgun to keep him company and because she wanted to support him, should he need any help.

Rosalie and two other cameramen, along with various other film crew flunkies, followed two different sets of hunters as they trekked along two separate trails through thick brush in the forest near Glacier National Park, on the trail of a man who was the subject of a statewide manhunt. Armed search teams had been brought together from all over northwest Montana. The hunters had been assigned a sector to search that morning in support of Sheriff Miller's deputies, after the sheriff had reached out the night before to ask for their help.

Brian had parked the van at a roadside rest stop

not far from the two trailheads, just a widening of the road with a concrete wall barrier between them and the drop into a deep ravine. He wore his new "pegs"—his nickname for what were actually pretty cool pieces of hardware. Andrew had been able to get them delivered sooner than the usual three weeks, because he'd mentioned that the manufacturer's work would be featured on the series, and the company had rushed the production schedule. He'd had a full four weeks to get used to them.

Brian still couldn't spend a full day in them, but he'd donned them right before heading out with the hunters to be their eyes and ears. Raydeen was there to remind him to remove the prosthetics and check his legs periodically for redness, although that requirement had stretched to two-hour intervals now. From the van, he'd monitor the team's livestream camera feeds as well as operate the drone in their sectors.

He'd already unboxed the drone, tested the camera, replaced the rechargeable battery, and was now ready to fly it. Picking up the van's remote, he opened the back door of the vehicle, set the drone in the middle of the floor, then sat at his console. The picture from the forward camera showed the open doorway and a clear view of the mountains inside the park.

All the calibrations on the left side of the screen were normal, so he used the joystick to start it. "We have liftoff," he murmured as it flew out the door.

BRIAN

"I have one of those—not as fancy, of course," Edgar said. "I take it out to Griffith Park on the weekends when I'm in LA. My kid loves to watch it fly, but I never share the controls. He tends to dive bomb people's heads."

Brian grinned. "We won't be doing any of that. I like to keep it high enough and moving fast enough that it doesn't get shot out of the air."

"Oh."

"You had to say that," Raydeen drawled from her seat beside him.

With the drone in the air, Brian hit the remote again and closed the back door of the van. Then he quickly scanned the monitors. The team all wore camera-outfitted helmets. He counted the number of feed "squares" on his large monitor, just to make sure they were all working, then turned his attention back to the drone.

Brian was happy to be part of another hunter op. While he'd done a few stakeouts since the one that had gotten him into trouble, simply watching houses to see whether skips turned up, he hadn't been needed for a true, track-a-thug-through-the-forest mission. Not since he'd begun wearing his new legs, anyway.

Brian was still getting used to them.

The first time he'd donned them, paying close attention to Andrew's guidance because he was eager to get this process conquered, he'd had a moment when he'd been helped by Raydeen and another therapist to stand on his new legs. The prosthetics had been fashioned to give him back the height he'd lost. When he'd straightened and gripped the parallel bars, he'd felt dizzy for a moment, and then he'd gazed *down* at Raydeen as she'd smiled teary-eyed back at him. "Damn, I feel like me again," he'd said, his voice hoarse with emotion.

Of course, that moment of euphoria had been followed by many more of frustration, because learning to walk when you couldn't feel your "feet" took some getting used to—a different kind of balancing act than any muscle memory could provide. However, he'd quickly moved from the parallel bars to a walker, and then crutches for support. These days, he used two canes with cuffs to help with his balance, but he hoped that, soon, he'd be competent enough to use just one, then someday none. His long-term goal was to learn to use prosthetics with running blades, so that he could get back to the kinds of exercise he'd enjoyed before his legs had been blown to hell. Now, that goal appeared to be within reach.

But today, the dual canes leaned against the work table. He'd left his chair at home. No, turning back. No letting it be "the crutch". Sure, he used it around his apartment a lot, but once he was dressed with his legs on, and was ready for work, he walked the hallway to the kitchen. Yes, his coffee cup was a thermos with a strap so he could hold it while he used his canes, but he was becoming more independent every day.

One of the coolest things for him was forgoing parking in a handicapped space and searching for a ramp. Although he was still a little wobbly, if he took his time, stepping onto a curb while balancing on his crutches was doable.

Hell, one thing he hadn't anticipated was that people looked at him differently. Before, many folks he passed never made eye contact, or if they did, it was to deliver a kind smile. These days, they greeted him with full smiles, some even admiring, which seemed a little weird to him, but Raydeen said they were just reflecting his confidence back to him.

And she was right. He felt more confident, more *himself*. He couldn't wait for the day he could stride down the sidewalk, holding her hand.

There wasn't any space for doubt left in his heart about where this relationship was heading. Not anymore. He was in love. He loved everything about Raydeen Pickering—her sarcastic wit, her stubborn fierceness, her sensual spirit. That her face and body made him happy just looking at them and feeling them beneath his fingertips was a bonus. Good Lord, all she had to do was give him a smile that stretched her freckled skin across her nose and made her brown eyes glitter, and he was lost.

He hadn't told her he loved her yet. Not in words. He hoped she'd be patient just a little while longer. Then again, she'd never spoken those words either.

He'd worried about that, at first. Reaper, oddly, had been the one to put his worry to rest.

One morning, after all the skip assignments had been made and the hunters with their film crew shadows had departed, it was just him and Reaper.

Reaper had chucked his chin at Brian's prosthetics. "How's it goin', buddy?"

He'd smiled and sat back in his chair, his legs extended in front of him. "Pretty damn good." He pointed toward the canes. "Raye says I'm getting close to not needing them at all." He wrinkled his nose. "I thought I was in pretty good shape for a wheelchair guy—I worked with hand weights, did crunches, sit-ups, pullups, pushups, but it's...different. My ass and thighs get a workout with me just standing in them. No amount of resistance, stretchy-band workouts prepares you for that."

"Good to know, but I wasn't talking about your legs. We can all see your progress, and we're proud of you. You've worked damn hard. I'm wondering how you and Raye are doin'."

"Great," Brian had said, but from the look Reaper gave him, a penetrating stare, he felt a frisson of doubt. "At least, I think so."

Reaper had grunted. "Not to get into your business..."

"No, it's okay, man." Brian sat forward in his chair. "I'm okay with advice or any observations. I'm not exactly an Einstein when it comes to relationships."

Reaper chuckled. "Me neither, but I will give you one little nugget of advice. Women like to be appreciated outside of the bedroom. They like hearing the words. Doesn't have to be mush and flowers; it can be a simple thank you, or *How was your day?*" Reaper cleared his throat. "Have you told her how you feel?"

"How I feel?" Okay, now that made him a bit uncomfortable.

"Not whether your stumps are sore or you have a cold, dumbass. How you feel," he said, knocking his fist against his chest, right over his heart. "Women like to know. But don't fuck it up by blurting it out when you're six inches deep. Tell them when they know you're not looking at 'em with sex-goggles on."

Brian had to crimp his lips together at that word. "Sex-goggles?"

Reaper rolled his eyes. "You know what I mean. Tell Raydeen when you're alone and not doing anything special. Or maybe, make it special, by cooking her a meal or rubbing her back when she's tired. Tell her you love her. You do, don't you?"

Brian nodded slowly. Of course, he did, but didn't Raydeen already know? Then again, she hadn't said those words to him. "She's never said how she feels."

"She probably doesn't want to scare you off. If she says 'I love you' too soon, she might be afraid you'll feel like she's pushing you to say it back."

"Or maybe she doesn't feel that way about me." That thought made his stomach hurt.

"You think she's only into you for the sex?"

"It's pretty great sex," Brian said, arching a brow.

Reaper shook his head. "I'm no expert about love, but then again, I don't have to be—I still know more than you. Raydeen's in love with you. Ain't no way she's not. Think she stalks every wounded vet like she did you? Besides, Carly says it's plain as the nose on your face. If the women think so, it's gotta be true. It's like they all have an internal love detector."

Brian was pleased Carly had said so. And he was with Reaper, if the women thought it was true, maybe they'd already squeezed Raydeen for the intel.

Reaper leaned back again. "Yeah, women don't come with a user's manual to tell us how to win their hearts. Part of the challenge for us men is to figure out what matters to them."

"Be a damn sight easier if there was a user manual," Brian muttered.

"Don't I know it. You know what I did? Just to prove how much I cared? I made her a damn koi fish pond. *In Montana.*" He shook his head. "Really had to study up how to do it right. Couldn't have goldfish icicles the first winter storm, but you should have seen her face when I took her outside to see it..." His gaze wandered and a smile curved his mouth.

Brian frowned. "I don't think Raye wants a koi fish pond."

"That is the mystery, man. The one you have to solve. What does Raye want?"

Brian still hadn't figured out exactly what great gesture he could make to prove how he felt. Words were cheap. He'd watched how the other hunters had proved their love.

Dagger let Lacey cover his face in mud masks for her YouTube vlog. Quincy was busy outfitting a nursery in his house, even though Tamara wasn't in any particular hurry to have babies. He just wanted to be ready, to prove to her he was in this thing for the long haul. Cochise showed Sammy all the time how much he respected and loved her. He was a big brother to her sister, had outfitted her room at college with everything a student needed, and he'd paid for her books. Sky had given Jamie the unfussy wedding she'd wanted, mud and all, free of all the frou-frou things she despised about weddings. Hook? He was pretty sure that Hook had proven his love when he'd believed in Felicity when all the evidence of the robberies at her former place of employment had pointed at her. She'd needed to be part of the team to catch the robber, and he'd enabled that.

So, what the hell could he do for a fiercely independent woman who didn't want koi ponds or need him to subject himself to the humiliation of mud masks for the world to see?

His mind went round and round that question while he flew the drone and watched the screens.

"Hey," Raydeen said, pointing at the drone's feed.

"Did you see that?"

He used the joystick to turn the drone back the way it had flown while he watched the camera feed. It still being winter, the forest canopy wasn't so thick he couldn't see breaks between the branches.

"There," she said again. "I see someone."

So did he. A pop of red amid the browns, greens, and grays.

He checked the elevation and brought the drone down so that it skimmed the treetops.

"Could that be your guy?" Edgar whispered.

Brian hit the zoom button to get a better look at the tall, burly man walking through the forest. He wore a red flannel jacket, dark pants, a ballcap that hid his face, and a backpack. Just as the drone passed him, the man glanced upward. Brian froze the screen and zoomed closer.

He glanced down at the desk at the mug shot of Chester Morgan, who was wanted for shooting up a bar in Hungry Horse, hospitalizing three men, and then leading law enforcement officials on a high-speed chase along Highway 2. When deputies had managed to get in front and in back of him and forced him to a stop, he'd killed one deputy, wounded the other, and then entered the woods.

Every law enforcement entity in Montana was hunting the man. And here he was, miles from the spot where he'd first left the road—and he wasn't very far from the teams' locations.

Brian radioed Reaper. "We spotted him. How far

from the highway are you guys?"

Brian couldn't drive crazy fast to meet the teams along the roadside, not with Edgar working the drone controls and tracking Chester's movements. As well, Raydeen gave constant updates regarding the location of the teams as she tracked them on an app on Brian's phone.

He slowed the van just as Reaper's team left the tree line.

The team crowded into the back of the van, leaving behind all of Rosalie's film crew, except the camera man, and then they were off again, making their way two more miles down the highway to find Dagger's group.

Once they had all the hunters and a pared down film crew packed like sardines inside the van, Edgar provided Raydeen the coordinates for Chester's current location, and Reaper called the sheriff to have him notify all the other agencies that they were closing in.

"The highway runs parallel to his route," Reaper said, leaning over Brian's shoulder. "We'll drop Dagger's team behind him, in case he doubles back, and then I'll need you to drop my team ahead of him. We'll squeeze him between us and surround him."

"He's running pretty close to the highway," Brian said. "I wonder if he's got someone ready to pick him up roadside."

"Could be," Reaper said. "Maybe you need to get a second drone in the air. One to watch the highway and see if anyone comes along, and the other following him."

"Good idea. Edgar there," he said, giving Edgar a glance in his rearview mirror, "can operate one while I work the other. He's not getting any filming done, but he's been really handy."

Edgar laughed. "I duct-taped my camera to the table. I'll salvage something."

"Great," Brian said, his tone dry.

They reached a spot just behind Chester's location, and Brian popped the back door for Dagger's team to exit. He watched as they ran into the forest, heading on a diagonal azimuth to hopefully catch up to killer.

Then Brian drove again, stopping when they were half a mile ahead of Chester.

Reaper patted his shoulder. "See you when this is through. Let us know if we get any company."

"Will do."

As soon as Reaper's team was in the woods, Brian turned the van around to head to where he'd noted a widening in the road a quarter of a mile back. When he parked there, he turned to Raydeen. "We'll be watching the action on the ground. I'll need you to keep an eye on the highway. Watch through your windshield and the mirrors. Might want to sit in my seat."

She nodded. "Anything suspicious, and I'll holler."

He leaned toward her, gave her a quick kiss, then grabbed the tops of the seat and used his hand on the table for balance as he walked to his seat in front of the monitors.

"You still got Chester in your sights?" he murmured to Edgar.

"Gonna need to take these controls?"

"Yeah, I'll need to coordinate the teams' movements once they're close. The other drone is in a case in the bench compartment nearest the door. Get it out, and we'll set it up, then you can work that remote controller."

A few minutes later, he and Edgar sat side by side, watching the views from the cameras as the drones flew over the highway and the forest.

"Reminds me of my college days," Edgar said.

"How's that?"

"I spent weekends playing online games with other players. This doesn't feel any more real than that was." He gave Brian a sideways glance and grinned. "This is fun."

"Maybe you missed your calling, man."

Edgar laughed. "Maybe I did. Although watching so many moving parts at once is a skill set I don't think I have."

Brian glanced at the bright dots on the GPS screen which indicated the team member's locations then double-checked Chester's location. "Dagger," he said into the mic, "He's over that next ridgeline in front of you. He's skirting it midway down the slope."

"Can you see if he's armed?"

"Have to assume he is, but I'll move closer..." He hovered the drone and dropped its elevation. Then he zoomed in on Chester from the back. "He has a rifle on one shoulder. Looks like something else holstered on his thigh.

At just that moment, Chester halted and glanced behind him and up.

"He's spotted the drone." When Chester raised his arm, he held a handgun. The gun jerked in his hand.

"Shot fired," Dagger said into his mic.

"Yeah, he was aiming at the drone, which was stupid. No accuracy at that distance. Now, he's running. He knows he has company. Good news is, he's running straight for Reaper's team. Maybe one click away from your location, Reaper."

"Roger that," Reaper said. "We'll hunker down and be waiting."

Tension inside the van rose.

He glanced at Raydeen. She was chewing a nail as she kept her gaze on the highway in front of them.

Edgar's eyes were wide as his gaze darted back and forth from his screen, which showed the highway, to Brian's screens.

For himself, Brian felt pretty cool. Yes, his focus was narrowing, just like it had in any combat scenario he'd found himself in the desert. His heart thudded at a steady beat. His breaths deepened. He heard a tapping and realized the sneaker on one of his artificial feet was making the noise.

Again, he checked Reaper's team's location. All the bright dots had halted; likely everyone had taken cover under brush or behind a tree.

Dagger's was keeping apace of Chester's progress, but not closing in as they had before. "Reaper, your team will make contact first. He's nearly there."

"See him," Cochise said. "I have a bead on him. I can take him out, if need be."

The sounds of heavy breathing in microphones filled the van. No one spoke.

Above the trees, the drone tracked Chester, until he halted then slowly turned in a circle. He raised the hand not holding the gun to his face.

"He knows you're there," he said quietly into the mic. "And I think he must have a two-way radio. I think he's talking to someone."

"Hey, Brian?"

Raydeen's voice broke his concentration, but he didn't dare look away from the screen. "Yeah, babe?"

"We've got company..."

He shot a quick glance out the front windshield just in time to see an older model SUV pull to a halt in the center of the highway. One window rolled down, the long barrel of a rifle appearing in the opening.

CHAPTER 12

Raydeen gasped when a large, firm hand wrapped around her upper arm and pulled her from her seat to the floor. She landed hard on her shoulder, but the sound of a gunshot and the thwack of a round hitting the windshield obliterated any thought of pain.

Brian still sat in his chair, but he was bent over her. "Keep on the floor," he whispered.

His glance went to Edgar, who had already moved to the floor even while he still held his drone controller. "Stay down."

"No problem," the man said. "But what the hell are we gonna do?"

Brian reached over Raydeen and tapped the latch on one of the lockboxes in the bench. He pulled out a long rifle and a large magazine filled with bullets, which he promptly inserted into the rifle. Then he pushed up to his full height, unable to crouch as he walked toward the back of the van.

"What the hell do you think you're doing?" Raydeen said. "You need to get down."

"I will," he said, opening the back door of the van, and then grimacing as he held onto the door and leaped to the ground.

Of course, he landed on his ass. "Motherfucker," he gritted out.

Raydeen scrambled on her hands and knees to get to the back and see whether he was hurt.

"Uh, three men just got out of that SUV," Edgar said behind her.

Her heart pounded in a chest suddenly too tight to breathe. "Brian, what the fuck are you doing?" she whispered harshly, as she glanced down to where he'd landed, only he was on his hands and knees now, still grasping the rifle.

He looked up at her. "Baby, get back inside. Lock the doors. Keep close to the floor. Please, I'll do what I can. Dagger's team heard what's happening. They're on the way. I just have to hold these guys off long enough..." He tightened his jaw.

She knew there wasn't time. That he had to try to save them. He was a soldier. He knew what to do.

Still, he needed to know. They'd danced around whatever it was they'd been doing long enough. "Don't get your ass killed, you hear? I love you."

His lips twitched, and then he flattened his body to the ground and crawled beneath the van.

Knowing she needed to keep safe, for his sake as well as her own, she slammed the door shut then moved toward the monitors, watching the feeds transmitting from the helmets worn by Dagger's team as they crashed through brush to get to them.

So far as Brian was concerned, the men in the SUV were chicken shits and didn't have a clue how to go about charging the van. They seemed to be arguing about who should take the lead as they ducked behind the open doors of their vehicle.

He thought maybe they needed a little more confusion to increase their agitation with each other, so he gazed down the long barrel of his rifle and selected his target—one of the SUV's tires. He drew a deep breath, let it partially out, then slowly pulled the trigger.

The tire deflated, and the men cursed.

"Uh, Chester's nearing the road, guys," Edgar's voice came over the comms.

"How far out are we?" Dagger said, his breaths huffing.

"You're right behind him. Can't tell how far, but you're closer than Reaper's team."

"I shot out a tire. We have three tangos on the road," Brian said.

"Good one, Bri," Reaper said, not sounding out of breath in the least. "Pin them down. We'll be there."

One of the men must have drawn the short

straw, because he moved swiftly from behind a door and ran toward the van, a handgun held out in front of him. His buddies formed a V-pattern behind him. They were a hundred yards from the van, and Brian knew he couldn't let them get any nearer. Keeping close to the van's left front wheel for cover, he took aim again, this time at a meaty thigh.

The man in the lead toppled over, screaming as he held his leg.

The other two fanned out.

Because he wanted to make sure the downed man was out of the fight for good, he took aim at his right shoulder.

Now, Brian knew he'd be more vulnerable, unable to keep watch on the two remaining targets as the drew nearer and split, so he chose one, the man coming toward his left side.

Scooting back just a bit to get behind the wheel, he moved his rifle and took aim, this time picking a larger body part—something he wouldn't miss—the right-side chest of the man crouched and running toward him. He pulled the trigger, knew he'd hit the man when he went to his knees, and then he moved back farther beneath the van, scooting out from under it because the remaining attacker had arrived at the front and was making his way around the right side.

Brian sat, his weapon raised, listening to the crunch of gravel.

Suddenly, from his right, Chester burst out of the tree line.

Brian moved out of his line of fire, scooting perilously close to the corner where the other man lurked.

"Get in the fucking truck," Chester yelled.

The man on the other side of the SUV paused.

"Tire's shot out! We need the van!" one of the fallen men called out. "I'm shot, Chester. Don't leave me behind."

Chester ran toward the van, passing his buddy. "Dumb fuckers. Why'd you engage in the first place?"

"We saw the antennas on the van," the fallen man wheezed. "Knew it was law enforcement. Knew they'd run us down if we didn't take 'em out."

"Why the hell would they know you're with me?" Chester bellowed. "Stupid fuckers!"

As quietly as he could, Brian pushed up from the ground, one hand on the van for balance. His right leg throbbed from the jump, but he ignored it. He figured the men wouldn't shoot the van on purpose because they needed it to escape, so Raydeen and Edgar were relatively safe for the moment, but he had to distract them again.

"They're signaling with their hands," Edgar whispered. "You hear me, Brian?"

Brian didn't answer, the other man was too close. Gritting his teeth, he moved away from the van, walking away in jerking motions as fast as he could, knowing he was revealing himself, but he had to make it to the ditch. If he could, he'd take up a position to continue to cause them problems.

He heard a distant rattle, like maybe Chester had tried the door handle of the van.

A crunch sounded behind him, but he was almost there. He raised a leg and jumped.

A shot fired, and he knew he was hit from the thud against his shoulder and the sudden fiery pain. Sliding down the side of the embankment, he reached out and grasped a rock, holding tight to stop his descent, and then rolled to his belly and brought up his rifle.

Gravel crunched closer; he shouldered his weapon and waited. The instant he saw a hand holding a gun appear over the edge, he drew his breath. When a face appeared to take a quick glance, he fired.

RAYDEEN PRESSED both hands over her mouth to keep from screaming. She'd watched the monitor Edgar had trained on Chester as he'd left the tree line, as well as the one pointed forward as the last of the three assailants from the SUV made his way to the van.

Then she'd heard Chester and the last man shouting to each other, and then listened as footsteps crunched beside the van.

Edgar had sat huddled beside her on the floor,

still operating his drone, watching the team as they converged, but they were only now reaching the road.

She'd heard the shot fired on the far side of the van, knew that was where Brian was, but she hadn't heard him cry out. Hadn't heard another sound. Fearing he'd been killed, all she could do was blink like crazy because tears were spilling from her eyes, and she couldn't take her gaze from the screens.

He can't be dead. He can't. I just told him I love him. The bastard has to say it back.

"They're here," Edgar whispered.

He pointed toward the row of monitors.

Dagger's team was moving from the tree line, weapons raised. In the distance, the drone caught the sight of flashing lights from many patrol cars and black sedans.

"Fly over the van, Edgar," she said. "I have to see."

Edgar blew out a breath and turned the drone to follow the law enforcement vehicles as they drew nearer to the van parked on the side of the road and the dark SUV that still sat sideways in the middle.

She picked out the two figures lying prone on the highway. Both men had their arms outstretched, away from their weapons.

Beside the van stood Chester, raising his hands high, a handgun gripped in one.

On the other side of the van, she saw a man laying over the edge of the road, and beneath him...

Brian glanced up at the drone and waved, but she

couldn't cheer. He was hurt. Blood covered his face and shoulders. She couldn't sit a moment longer. While figures on the screen began to move in to capture Chester, she pushed open the back of the van, jumped to the ground, and ran for the embankment.

Once there, she nearly vomited. The man lying over the edge barely had a head. Stepping past him, she went down on her butt and scooted down the side over slimy leaves and mud, her gaze going to Brian who gave her a weak smile. "Hey, babe," he said.

"Hey, babe, my ass!" she gritted out, and then hiccuped as she crawled sideways to get to him. "Oh my God, Brian, are you hurt?" She reached out for him, but he thrust out his right arm to hold her away.

"Baby, don't. I'm covered in blood and brains."

She drew off the green sweater he so loved and began to wipe his face and hair.

He leaned back against the dirt and gravel. "I wanted to make it special. The right moment, you know?"

"What are you talking about?" she said, frowning as she noted the slow seepage of blood running from his bent elbow. Was he woozy from blood loss? "You need to sit forward. I have to find the wound."

"Shut up, Raye."

"What did you say?" she said, giving him a glare. Was he really trying to get her pissed when she was trying to save his life?

"Just. Please. A second." He sighed and took a

deep breath. "I love you."

"I know, asshole. Now, will you please lean forward?"

"You know?" he said, a faint smile curving the corners of his lips.

"Of course, I know. You haven't given me any shit when I made you work hard, no matter how much you hurt. And you just risked your life to save mine. Of course, I know."

He got his elbows under him and began to push away from the ground. "Glad that's over," he said, his voice sounding ragged.

"Was it such a fucking ordeal, telling me you love me? Am I that scary?"

"Sometimes. I love that about you."

Her eyes stung with tears, but she blinked them away and leaned around him to check for wounds. Blood burbled from a small round hole in his shoulder. Her stomach lurched, and she began to shake. "For a big tough guy, that asshole must have used a twenty-two. Thank God."

"Yeah, guess I should be happy about that," and then he groaned because she'd pressed hard against the wound with her sweater.

Fear and anger boiled together inside her. How could he be so calm when he was bleeding out? Didn't he know how much his life mattered? "Think I'm gonna go easy on you because you got your ass shot—"

Brian shut her up with a hard kiss.

EPILOGUE

THE DAY BRIAN was released from the hospital, the hunters gathered at the office building. He'd insisted on walking inside, so Raydeen followed closely in case he needed help, but he managed quite well on one hard-handled crutch. He'd undergone more rehab while he'd been in the hospital, endless walks down the corridors, which had helped him regain his progress and then some.

Raydeen couldn't be prouder of him as he stood inside the entrance and gazed at the big dark blue banner with the MBH logo that stretched above the counter and said, "Welcome home, Brian!"

A crooked smile spread across his face as he gazed at his friends. Fletch Winter, the owner of the agency, was there as well to greet him. They all clapped as he strode confidently around the counter and into the bullpen.

The women gave him gentle hugs, the men

clapped his uninjured shoulder. After they'd had their cake and daiquiris—Lacey's contribution—they all settled into seats.

Fetch cleared his throat. "We're thinking you might need to expand the building a bit."

Brian gave him a questioning glance.

"Can't bring a woman home to live with you in a two-room apartment," Reaper said. "We've been drawing up plans."

"Wouldn't it be easier for us to simply find a house?" Brian said, his gaze going to Raydeen, because he had broached the subject with her while he was still in the hospital.

She'd been noncommittal because she'd known about the hunters' plan.

"We're spoiled," Jamie said, drawing his attention. "We like having you here, watching over the place while we're scattered to the winds."

"And Raydeen said you like your mornings, getting ready then making your way into the office," Reaper said. "If you're not burdened by being tied to this place, we'd like to show you what we've got planned. You'd have privacy, more space, but you'd still have access to the office."

Brian's smile stretched wide. "I like my administrative duties, and it is pretty convenient when some of you are out for me to wander down the hall to help out with any needed research."

"Doesn't mean you'll be tied to the office all the time," Fetch said. "As well as you're getting around, I expect you'll be doing more knocking on doors to find skips."

"But you'll have a partner," Reaper interjected.

Brian's eyebrows rose. "Are we hiring again?"

"Brand newbie, who needs to learn the ropes," Lacey said, grinning.

When Brian's gaze scanned the room, it landed on Raydeen who couldn't help giggling. "I'm joining the gang." She arched a brow. "That is, if you can stand to work with me, day in-day out. I'm pretty good with paperwork. Know my way around Microsoft Office. I'm told I have a talent for getting people to tell me their deepest secrets..."

"I can vouch for that one," Brian said. "You sure? What about your work with Soldiers' Sanctuary?"

"My work's here, baby. Looking after you."

His eyebrows lowered. "You saying I need a babysitter?"

"No, I'm saying, you need someone to tell you when you're being a jackass."

"Oh boy, here they go again," Reaper mumbled.

"Hey, Bri," Lacey said, holding up her hand. "Rosalie sent a rough cut of your segment. Want to watch it?"

Brian blew out deep breath. "Anyone make popcorn?"

Laughter sounded, and Carly, Lacey, and Dagger moved to the kitchen.

When popcorn and sodas had been distributed, Reaper dimmed the lights. They took seats huddled around Brian's large monitor, and he hit PLAY on the screen.

As a narrator described the special segment and gave a plug for donations to the Soldiers' Sanctuary, Raydeen reached for Brian's hand. They were going to be okay. And the expansion wasn't charity. Reaper had been adamant about needing Brian happy and here, because the office went to hell when he wasn't. When he'd offered her a job as well, and then offered to help with her training, she'd taken only a minute before making her decision.

Sure, she'd been scared to death out on the highway with Chester Morgan and his goons moving in on them, but she hadn't lost her shit until she'd thought Brian had been shot. What he did was different every day, every skip providing a new challenge. She was pretty sure she'd love the work and love working with Brian. And while she was at his side, she'd make damn sure he didn't do anything stupid, ever again. Like getting himself shot, trying to save her. Next time, she'd be armed and ready to take care of her own damn self. Because that was the kind of wife she planned to be.

Not that Brian had asked. Yet. Maybe, she wouldn't wait for him to pop the question. Maybe she'd do it herself. She'd give him a little time, but if he was feeling too cozy with their arrangement and kept waiting for that "special" moment, she'd ask him when she was riding his fine-ass cock, unable to say anything but yes.

BRIAN

She smiled at the thought and glanced at him.

He was looking right back, his eyes narrowed.

Yikes, she wondered if he'd read her expression.

As the film detailed Brian's journey from a description of how he'd been injured, including photographs of him at Walter Reed, through his first halting steps in his new prosthetics, to the moment Edgar filmed him from the top of the embankment while Raydeen knelt in her bra, trying to staunch Brian's blood with her sweater, her heart grew and grew until her chest felt tight from all the warm emotions swirling inside her. Damn, she loved this man.

She would marry a brave man. A man no longer wounded by what his body had experienced. As terrifying and terrible as those minutes on the highway had been, they'd proved to him that he was still a soldier, still a man.

As the narrator repeated the Soldiers' Sanctuary pitch at the very end, Brian leaned sideways toward her. "How soon do you think Andrew can hook me up with running blades?" he whispered.

Raydeen laughed. "I think after he sees how cute he looked on TV, he'll fit you in this week."

Brian squeezed her fingers. "Thank you, Raye."

She turned her head to meet his gaze. "For what, baby?"

"For giving me back myself."

She shook her head. "That was all you. You just

had to be ready. All you needed was a kick in the ass."

He gave her a one-sided smile. "Baby, don't talk about asses."

"And...that's our cue to leave..." Reaper said.

Raydeen and Brian didn't notice as everyone faded away. The front door chimed, but they couldn't have cared less. When Raydeen straddled Brian as he sat on a rolling desk chair and shimmied down his cock, he pressed a kiss between her breasts then hugged her close against him. "I love you," he said.

"I love you more."

"Not possible," he said, his voice muffled because he was nibbling on a nipple.

She gripped his hair and tilted back his head. "Are we gonna argue? *Now?*"

Brian cupped her bottom then gave one side a slap. "No better time. I've got you all figured out. The hotter you get under the collar, the hotter the sex."

"I'm not wearing a damn collar." But she couldn't hide her grin as she gripped his ears and bent to kiss him. The man thought he had her all figured out, but a girl couldn't leave a guy feeling too smug. She had a surprise or two ready to spring. One which would arrive in about eight months' time... And oh, she couldn't wait to see his face.

Would he laugh or cry? Would he be as happy as she was? As scared? She couldn't wait to share the news, but first, they had to get the business of getting married out of the way.

Just as she began to hum with pleasure, moving up and down his shaft, Brian gripped the notches of her hips and held her hard against him.

She bent her face toward his and gave him a glare. "Not the time. I gotta move."

"And I'll let you, but you have to answer one question—and if you don't give me the answer I want—we're gonna sit here, just like this."

She rolled her eyes. "Ask the question, already. But if it's about the blowjob I promised you in the hospital, you don't have to ask."

Brian pressed his lips together. "Shut up, Raye."

"I really don't like that phrase." But she really did, because he only used it when he gave her that fierce, sexy look he was giving her now.

He pressed a finger against her lips.

She moved her lips against the finger and gave a garbled, "Think you can hold me down with just one hand?"

"Damn, you're stubborn." He gripped the back of her neck and brought her down for a hard kiss. When he pulled back his head, he blurted, "Will you marry me?"

She drew a sharp breath. "'Bout damn time, daddy."

DREAM OF ME

UNCHARTED SEALS

New York Times and *USA Today* Bestselling Author
Delilah Devlin

UNCHARTED SEALS

DREAM
OF ME

NEW YORK TIMES BESTSELLING AUTHOR
DELILAH DEVLIN

CHAPTER 1

DREAD WEIGHED HER DOWN, *making her feel sluggish and stupid.* I have to find the right door. *She stumbled into a long corridor, wood paneling below wainscoting, and tattered, dark teal wallpaper with faded pink roses above. Like she'd seen in her grandmother's house when she was a child. Only this corridor was endless and lined with teakwood doors—all identical, all closed.*

How could she possibly find the right one? The panic in her body made her want to run and try them all, but she knew she didn't have much time—a lesson she'd already learned. And turning the wrong knob led to horrors best left unknown.

She wanted to run but couldn't, because her feet were as heavy as lead, mired in invisible muck, slowing her steps, making her tired. Her stride shortened. She dragged her feet on the floral carpet, staticky sounds following her, sparks biting her naked ankles.

At last, she came to a halt, her body swaying. Too tired to care what she might find, she opened the door...

AISLIN DUPREE TUGGED at the collar of her dark uniform. She'd have a rash—a rosy red ring around her neck—because she'd sweated so much the collar was stiff.

"Stop messin' with it, Ash," her partner drawled from the driver's seat. "You'll only make it worse."

"This stickiness is making me crazy. Heat's so bad I wonder why I bother taking a shower before shift. I'm drenched again before I'm dressed. And why aren't you sweating?"

She watched as Marc LeBrun's smile in profile stretched in that lazy way that never failed to make her tingle from head to toe and exciting all the sexy parts in between.

He made a turn before glancing her way, flashing a smile. "I don't fidget. Chillax, baby. It's just another mornin' in easy town. Good times..."

Good times... His sly code for sex whenever they were in company. "Stop," she said, holding up her hand. "That's not helping."

He chuckled, but kept his gaze on the road ahead. "You think about Grand Isle?"

"Fishing on Grand Isle is not my definition of a sexy getaway."

"Won't be no fishin', sugar. Just you 'n' me. Bed and breakfast on the beach."

"The sight of oil rigs kinda spoils the view," she grumbled, but only half-heartedly. The thought of getting away from the city, which smelled foul this time of year, due to the rain and humidity and the sewage floating just beneath the street grates, did sound good. "Should just head to Thibodeaux. Nice hotels there. Might find one with room service. We can take an airboat ride into the swamps if we get bored..." she said, giving him a teasing, sideways glance.

"And that's sexier than a B&B on the beach?" His chuckles grew and grew.

And she grinned, happy she was there beside him. Just another day on their beat. Most cops rode single, but this part of town was more dangerous. Extra manpower had been added to the shifts in this ward. They'd been paired now for six months. Lovers for the last three.

However they spent their time together didn't really matter. It was always...good times.

Dispatch broke the silence with the code for robbery. "Be advised, female at location says pedestrian forced her to empty her register."

The location was only five blocks away. Marc gave her a short nod and flipped on the lights.

Ash pressed the button on the mic. "51-12 responding. Five minutes to location."

"51-12. 10-4. All units in the vicinity be on the lookout for a male, medium height, wearin' a gray hoodie..."

The next few minutes passed in a blur. They arrived at the shop with its barred windows and shabby, white-washed exterior.

Marc entered first with his weapon drawn. "This is NOPD," he called out.

No response came from inside.

Ash edged closer to his body, turning to watch their six. The hair on the back of her neck rose. She knew Marc felt it too because, for once, he was quiet and moving slowly.

The shop was small, just a twenty by twenty square filled with rows of racks stocked with snack foods and drinks. Glancing over the top of the racks, Ash spotted a door toward the back, partially open. Dark.

Both officers crouched down behind the racks as they made their way steadily toward the darkened doorway.

Marc pointed down an aisle, indicating she should come at the door from another angle.

Keeping her breathing even, she nodded and sped silently to the end of the row.

Another nod, and she moved with her back to the wall, easing toward the doorway. From this angle, she could see the bottom of a dirty sneaker, unmoving on the floor.

She lifted her finger and pointed to the door, indicating she saw one person. When they stood flanking the door, she reached out an arm to open it wider, a loud creak sounding in the silence. It thudded softly against the wall of the small office.

Marc edged around the corner, stepped over the young woman on the floor and went to the door at the far side of the room, which stood wide open, sunlight streaming inside from the alley.

Ash bent over the young woman and placed a hand on her chest, felt movement, and then pressed her mic to call for an ambulance. But behind her, she heard another creak and stiffened.

Marc swung around, his weapon raised. "Get down!" he shouted.

Ash ducked toward the woman, not wanting to get in Marc's line of fire. Above her, a loud blast boomed—a shotgun round. Her body stiffened, and she glanced toward Mark. Blood burst from multiple places on his face and neck, spraying outward. His arms flung wide.

She screamed and came up, swinging back with her elbow and connected with hard muscle. No time to think. No time to pray. Marc had to be okay. She had to get to him. But first, she had to live.

As she turned, something struck her cheek. She went down, watching as though in slow motion as a man in a hoodie raised a gun and pointed it at her. Her own weapon entered her line of sight. A loud explosion sounded, the recoil jolting her arm. He jerked, his arms going limp, dropping the shotgun, and then he lurched past her, stepping on Marc as he exited through the door.

She got back to her knees and crawled toward Marc who lay so still, too quiet. His face was a mess, blood dripping down both sides into his thick black hair, pockets of flesh gone. What worried her most was the sluggish pulsing river flowing from his neck wound. She pressed her hands over it and leaned toward him. "Marc, hang on, baby. I'm here. I'm here."

He didn't blink. Didn't move.

She pressed harder with one hand and lifted the other to her radio. "108. Officer down. Officer down. Shots fired." She knew her voice sounded ragged, strained. They'd know the situation was bad. *Please come fast.*

She fought to control her panic. Do her job. Again, she pressed the button to let them know the suspect was fleeing the scene. "Six-feet-four male, gray hoodie, jeans, sunglasses. On foot." She released the button and let the mic hang from her shoulder as she bent over Marc, all her concentration going now to her partner who was dying. She knew he was. Her chest pinched, and she could barely breathe. No miracle would save him.

And then...a hand touched her shoulder. "Ma'am, let me help. I'm a doctor."

She glanced to the side, shock making her quiver. "Save him, please."

A kind face beneath a shock of thick gray hair entered her vision. "I'll do what I can."

As she side-stepped on her knees down Marc's

prone body to make room, she shook her head, feeling like she was falling, like she was about to faint. Black spots danced before her eyes. "No, no. This isn't what happened. That didn't happen," she said, her voice sounding from far away.

The doctor glanced at her with cold blue eyes. "Isn't this what you wanted to happen?"

Ash took a deep breath then shot a glance at Melanie Oats, the psychologist she'd been required to see since the shooting.

"The dream was different this time?" Melanie asked, fingers steepled beneath her chin.

Why had she confided the fact she'd been having nightmares? She was getting tired of reliving Marc's death. "It's always different. In little ways," Ash muttered. "But this time, I felt hope. That doctor appearing. That didn't happen in actuality." She took a deep breath and pressed her lips together. "Didn't really matter. He didn't change a damn thing."

The woman's expression remained a professional mask. "Did you expect that his arrival would...change something...?"

Ash couldn't meet her gaze. If Ash told her that some folks she knew believed dreams weren't just something brains concocted to help work people through problems, that dreams could be doorways into other worlds, the therapist might wonder if Ash believed that, too. And Ash couldn't have Melanie doubting her mental state. She needed Melanie Oats's seal of approval, her report that gave her a clean bill of health so she could go back to work. A score needed to be settled.

That last thought made her go still. Her burning desire wasn't just for revenge against the skinny motherfucker who'd killed Marc; she wanted revenge against the whole dirty city. Better hide her anger, or Melanie Oats would never give her blessing.

The psychologist let out a breath and cupped her crossed knee. "You've never spoken about your family."

Hell no. "My *family* has nothing to do with this. With me."

"Do you understand why that would concern me?"

Ash grunted. Melanie Oats had never met her family.

"I can't approve you returning to work. To wearing a gun. Not yet." She pressed her lips together for a moment. "I think you should take my previous suggestions to heart. Take some time. Visit with family. Deal with the grief, instead of bottling it up. You won't talk to me. Maybe there's someone else you trust you can unburden yourself to."

The woman thought she should unburden herself? Did she even have the right to let go of her guilt? She'd been the one who'd opened that door, who hadn't looked behind it. Never mind the guy had to have been as skinny as a rail to fit in the narrow space. She shook her head to rid herself of the vision of that dark area behind the door. Every time she imagined it, the space was deeper and darker. Maybe the therapist was right. "All right. I'll take some time."

But she wouldn't go home. She'd handle this on her own. Like she'd handled every other problem she'd ever faced.

"Good. I'll see you in two weeks?"

Ash pushed up from her chair and gave the woman a vague nod. First order of business was finding a drink. Maybe several. Tomorrow, she'd do something for herself. She didn't want to continue this path. She had work to do. Maybe tomorrow she'd run along Wisner Trail beside Bayou St. John. She needed to keep fit. Needed honed strength to be ready the next time.

Is this what you wanted to happen?

What had that doctor in her dream meant? Yes, she'd wanted a miracle that day as she'd knelt in Marc's blood. She'd cursed and prayed for divine intervention, but a doctor with a dozen bags of blood at his fingertips still couldn't have saved him.

Or had he meant something else? Not that she'd wanted Marc to die, but that she had expected him to leave her at some point. Hadn't she always been waiting for the other shoe to drop in her relationship with Marc? In a flash, they'd fallen into lust and immediately into love. Too damn easy. Nothing good in her life had ever come that easily.

Ash pushed on the glass door and entered the

sidewalk, assailed by the heat and the street noises, the honking and shouts, the music in the distance. The therapist's office was on Canal, blocks away from the constant hubbub in the heart of the French Quarter. While seedy and dirty, the Quarter was filled with whores and tourists, but she never felt afraid there. There was a rhythm to the streets, a flow that seeped into her bones and had her swaying as she walked. Her strides were longer, her breaths deeper. The scent of liquor lured her, and she followed the curled fingers of a black man with an easy smile beckoning her at the open bar door, calling in the tourists. He didn't have to cajole her. She probably wore a desperate look.

She slid into the darkness, away from the sunlit door, and passed the band on a dais, taking a break to drink. Cigarette smoke wafted in from the street, following her, and she wished she hadn't quit years earlier, because she'd love nothing better than to drink and smoke herself into a stupor. But then she'd have to wander outside to puff. So fuck that.

"You back again?"

Ash glanced over her shoulder to see a woman with a long weave and two-inch ruby nails teeter toward her on impossibly high heels. "Got a problem with it?" But she gave Gennie a tired grin.

"Sugar, you can come back as often as you like, but what you need ain't in any bottle."

Someone else telling her what she needed. Ash rubbed a hand over her face. "What I need is to get back to work, and I can't do that because that bitch of a shrink won't let me."

"That bitch be doin' you a favor, hon." Her hand curved over Ash's shoulders, and she gave her a squeeze. "Go home," she said, leaning to speak into her ear, because the band had started tuning their instruments. "Jus' go home. What you need is rest. And family. Go see your Auntie."

Stiffening, Ash shook her head. "She'll only hang a gris-gris bag around my neck and tell me to make nice with the spirits. That isn't happening."

"What about that sister of yours?"

Ash shrugged. She and her half-sister weren't close. Hell, they hadn't known they were sisters until her father's bigamy came to light at his funeral. She'd known Siobhan when they were children. They'd shared the same classrooms, played together on the monkey bars, but their father's sin had pushed a wedge between their two families. Her mother's bitterness had ensured whatever friendship they'd had was set aside out of family loyalty.

Her "Auntie" was a woman she'd seen only rarely in their small town because she lived deep in the bayou. They'd become better acquainted when her own mother fell ill and no amount of pain medication could soothe her through the final stages of the cancer that finally killed her. Her mother had sent her into the bayou for a remedy.

Something that had shocked Ash, because she'd

known her mother was aware of Auntie Clare and the rumors that swirled around her.

But Ash'd made that trek, several times, bringing home herbs in a cheesecloth bag that she'd sprinkled into her mama's tea. The tea had done its job, giving her comfort at the last, ensuring she maintained her dignity until the very end when she'd simply slipped away in her sleep.

At the funeral, Auntie—for she'd insisted on being called that—had been the one who held her hand throughout the service, while Siobhan had sat stiffly on the other side of her own mother.

Ash tossed back another shot and shook her head. "Gennie, I can't go home. There's nothing for me there." Her home was gone. Sold at her mother's death, and the funds used to pay her college tuition. And she'd never looked back. Never again spoken to Auntie or Siobhan.

At least Ash had New Orleans. The city was her friend. Not a good one. It had led her astray a time or two. But she was familiar. And never judged her. If Ash wanted to stay shit-faced for the next two weeks, no one would raise an eyebrow. Maybe she'd have to find another bar though for her bender.

Dark thoughts weighing her down, she paid for her drinks and left, winding her way through the quarter, away from the tourist center to a side street with two-storied houses hidden behind small courtyard entrances. At one gate, she pushed the latch and ambled through, her feet dragging over worn paving stones to the porch with an iron railing and the baby bougainvillea she'd been coaxing for months to wind around the porch rail. Didn't matter anymore. The next tenant might hate the fuchsia blooms. Her lease was up soon. And without Marc sharing the rent, she couldn't afford to stay. Not that she wanted to. Too many memories lay inside the house's walls.

She unlocked the front door and stepped over the threshold, kicking the door shut behind her and stepping over the pile of mail the mailman had dropped through the slot the past weeks. She supposed she should go through it in case a bill needed paying, but the thought slipped through her mind and faded in an instant as she passed the living room and headed straight to the kitchen.

Cheap scotch sat on the counter. Yesterday's tumbler beside it. She swished it clean with tap water, then poured a drink and headed back to the porch, to an overstuffed chair pulled close to the railing. She settled into the chair and set her feet on the rail, her drink resting on her belly as she stared between the branches of the old oak in the courtyard at the huge silver moon.

A breeze feathered her hair against her cheek. Almost like the light stroke of fingertips, and for a moment, she closed her eyes and allowed herself to imagine Marc's fingers on her skin.

But only for a moment, because in the next, a deep painful twinge tightened her chest. She took a sip of her drink, let the liquor burn its path down her throat, and then breathed deeply. *Why couldn't it have been me? I could have blocked the shot with my body if I hadn't dived over the clerk on the floor.*

If only I could go back and change it. I'd give anything. Please, God. Please.

A tear slipped down her cheek, and she sniffed then grimaced and wiped it away with the backs of her fingers. She'd cried enough. Doing so didn't change a thing. Only left her with a headache and grogginess. And she'd had enough of both.

Ash set her drink on the porch rail, dropped her feet, and stood, swaying a little. She'd thought she'd have to finish the rest of the bottle before sleep consumed her. Maybe not. She reentered the house and made to step over the mountain of mail.

Her body swayed again, and she knew she'd better get to a chair fast. Her foot kicked an envelope the size of an invitation with a beautiful island-themed stamp and sent it sliding over the old, weathered oak floor.

Nearer the kitchen now, she saw her name written in thick, terse pen strokes. A man's handwriting. Unfussy, bold. Rather like Marc's had been, although his scrawl had been nearly illegible.

Curious, she eased down beside the letter and picked it up. She carried the letter into the living room, to the leather couch she'd used as a bed since she'd come home alone that first night. She pulled an afghan around her shoulders and turned on the lamp on the table beside her to take a closer look. She slid a fingernail under the flap and opened it.

Aislin...

No "Dear Aislin", no "Dear Occupant"...

It was scam, right? One of those things where they made you think they knew you well, or knew your cousin or best friend at college, and they just hated to contact you, but they were stranded in Paris. Would you please send money? And if you were dumb enough to do it, you got hit with a huge credit card bill when some Ukrainian charged a Mercedes. Well good luck with that. Her credit card was nearly maxed out.

Or maybe the letter was one of those time-share things where she had to sit through a sales pitch...

She ought to toss it. But the trash can was all the way in the kitchen. And now, she was just a little bit curious.

The next line sat like a stone in her belly.

I'm a friend of Marc's. We have to talk.

Below that was a phone number with a note to call day or night.

Was this from another friend who'd just found out he'd been killed? Ash wasn't sure she could bear having that conversation even one more time. But she thought of Marc, and the fact he'd had a huge pool of friends, not only on the force, but from his time in the Navy SEALs. Blinking at the sudden burn in her eyes, she could almost hear him saying, "Don't wuss out now, Dupree."

So she rose, slid her phone from her back pocket, and quickly dialed the number before she did just that. Maybe she'd get an answering machine and could just hang up. Tomorrow, she'd forget about the urge that had her waiting as the phone rang.

She moved the phone away and raised her thumb to end her call, when she heard, "Ash, don't hang up," in a smooth deep voice.

Ash drew a swift breath but remained silent. How did he know the call was from her? And that voice—she'd felt a quiver ripple over her skin. His voice was a call to temptation, but she wasn't interested. "I'm sorry. I dialed the wrong number."

"Wait. Ash."

That was the second time he'd used her name. Her fingers tightened on her phone. "How do you know it's me calling?"

"Please, don't be afraid," came that deep voice. "Marc gave me your number, but I thought the note might be easier than another call from a stranger."

The stranger's voice was smoother yet again. "Marc's dead," she said, her voice more strident than she intended.

"Something I discovered a few days ago when I called the work number he'd given me. I'm very sorry for your loss."

The very words she didn't want to hear. Her throat tightened. "Well, thanks for that sentiment," she said in a rush, ready to end the call as quickly and politely as she could.

"Forgive me, but this may come as a shock. Marc made arrangements for a trip to a Caribbean island, reserved a cottage, and bought plane tickets. He wanted to spring the getaway on you. Said something about tricking you into thinking you were vacationing on Grand Isle. He didn't want you to know a thing until he drove up to the hangar where the plane would be waiting."

"Grand Isle…" Her hand tightened on her phone. "But he's gone, now," she said, tears welling. He'd planned a sexy getaway. Something special. Marc wasn't a romantic man, but he'd planned this?

"I'm glad you called. And I know it hasn't been all that long, but the trip is already paid for. Yours, whenever you have the time to get away. You'll have complete privacy, a house on the beach."

"I can't," she said, her voice scratchy as she fought tears. She angled her head upward and stared at the ceiling. "I have work," she lied.

"Like I said, any time you can travel. Everyone needs to get away some time, Ash."

He paused.

She was surprised she wished he'd say something else. Something about his voice was soothing, making her feel like she wasn't the only person in the world hurting. "Where is this island?"

"Western Caribbean. Just a hop from New Orleans. Let me know when you can come. I'll make all the arrangements."

She thought about what Melanie had said about

her getting away. Ash would prefer to take her vacation inside a bottle. But she couldn't be rude to Marc's friend. "How did you know him?"

"We were on the same team in the SEALs."

She nodded although she knew he couldn't see. Her gaze went to the couch with its natty afghans, and then swept the room where they'd spent evenings cuddling on the sofa while they watched Saints' games or the latest Avengers movie.

A chance to breathe air that wasn't stale. To see a room that didn't hold his imprint. To visit a place that they hadn't been as a couple. "How many days' reservation did he make?"

"A week."

Maybe seven days would be long enough to figure something out. Or simply to sleep without Marc's scent surrounding her. "I can come now."

Another pause.

Had she surprised him? Did he need more time? She hoped not. Here was a chance to bolt from their home. And she'd had just enough to drink to sustain her courage to leave.

"I'll make arrangements for a car to pick you up in half an hour."

Her body stiffened, and she blinked. That soon? "O-okay."

"Bye, Aislin."

The call ended, and she lowered her phone to stare at the screen. Was she really doing this? Panic fluttered in her belly, and she hovered her thumb over the screen, tempted to redial the number. But again, she stared at the sofa.

"I have to pack," she whispered. She'd cram clothes into a duffel and water the dying plants. Maybe if she kept moving, she wouldn't think, wouldn't change her mind.

And she needed to get away, to a place where the mirrors didn't reflect the places Marc had been. Relief washed like a cool wave through her. The card, the call...both seemed like a divine hand had reached down to offer a second chance.

As she climbed the stairs, she realized she'd never asked his name. She snorted. She wasn't worried about walking into a trap laid to kidnap lonely women. At twenty-nine, she was too old to be interesting to sex traffickers. Too tired to give a shit.

Take that back. Right about now, she'd love the hell out of a good fight.

ALSO BY DELILAH DEVLIN

Montana Bounty Hunters

Reaper (#1)

Dagger (#2)

Reaper's Ride (#3)

Cochise (#4)

Hook (#5)

Wolf (#6)

Animal (#7)

S*x on the Beach (related)

Big Sky Wedding

Quincy (#8)

Brian (#9)

Uncharted SEALs

Watch Over Me (#1)

Her Next Breath (#2)

Through Her Eyes (#3)

Dream of Me (#4)

Baby, It's You (#5)

Before We Kiss (#6)

Between a SEAL and a Hard Place (#7)

Heart of a SEAL (#8)

Hard SEAL to Love (#9)

Big Sky SEAL (#10)

Head Over SEAL (#11)

SEAL Escort (#12)

Texas Cowboys

Wearing His Brand (#1)

The Cowboys and the Widow (#2)

Soldier Boy (#3)

Bound & Determined (#4)

Slow Rider (#5)

Night Watch (#6)

Cowboys on the Edge

Wet Down

Controlled Burn

Cain's Law

Flashpoint

Triplehorn Brand

Laying Down the Law (#1)

In Too Deep (#2)

A Long, Hot Summer (#3)

Night Fall

Sm{B}itten (#1)

Truly, Madly…Deadly (#2)

Knight in Transition (#3)

Wolf in Plain Sight (#4)

Knight Edition (#5)

Night Fall on Dark Mountain (#6)

Frannie and the Private Dick (#7)

Sweet Succubus (#8)

Truly, Madly…Werely (#9)

Bad to the Bone (#10)

Long Howl Good Night (#11)

First Knight (#12)

Big Bad Wolf (#13)

Texas Billionaires Club

Tarzan & Janine (#1)

Something To Talk About (#2)

Who's Your Daddy (#3)

Love & War (#4)

∽

Some Standalone Stories

New Orleans Nights

Begging For It

Hot Blooded

Raw Silk

Warrior's Conquest

Rogues

Enslaved by the Viking Short Story

Conquests

Smokin' Hot Firemen

ABOUT DELILAH DEVLIN

Delilah Devlin is a *New York Times* and *USA TODAY* bestselling author with a reputation for writing deliciously edgy stories with complex characters. She has published nearly two hundred stories in multiple genres and lengths, and she is published by Atria/Strebor, Avon, Berkley, Black Lace, Cleis Press, Ellora's Cave, Entangled, Grand Central, Harlequin Spice, HarperCollins: Mischief, Kensington, Montlake Romance, Running Press, and Samhain Publishing.

You can find Delilah all over the web:
WEBSITE
BLOG
TWITTER
FACEBOOK FAN PAGE
PINTEREST

ABOUT DELILAH DEVLIN

Subscribe to her newsletter ***so you don't miss a thing!***
Or email her at: delilah@delilahdevlin.com

Made in United States
North Haven, CT
26 March 2024